D-DAY REPULSED

SMALL ARMS DECIDE THE FATE IN NORMANDY

CLAUDE STAHL

D-Day Repulsed

*Small Arms Decide
The Fate In Normandy*

Claude Stahl

Chapters

Lights Over the Dunes

Helmut tried to recognize the time on his wristwatch. *Just three hours until sunrise,* he thought. Through the binoculars, he saw only dark, black-gray clouds and dark lines on the horizon. The captain unexpectedly came by; he had two field glasses hanging around his neck. "Not today," he said calmly. Helmut remained skeptical. The old man meant that the enemy would not come today. *How did he know that?* The old ones of his squad, those over 30, had seemed tense during the last few days, as if they had felt something in their little finger. But if the captain said the attack wouldn't come today, who was Helmut to argue? He didn't have a nose for danger like this veteran did.

It was 1944, and the war had gone on much longer than anyone had expected, longer than anyone had hoped. Despite the fatigue that everyone seemed to be feeling, it was undeniable that something was coming—something big.

A gunman crawled out of the adjacent pillow-box, crept slowly toward Helmut, and handed him a cup. "Pure coffee; help yourself."

Without a word, Helmut nodded gratefully. *Really strong coffee beans.* That was not something taken for granted by the soldiers here on the Atlantic Wall in Normandy.

The clouds on the horizon seemed to clear; the night was no longer black. Was there just a short flash on the horizon? Nope. Nothing more to see. The flies began early today. Here on the dunes of Normandy, there were millions of flies; but they had left the men here more or less alone the last few days due to the wet weather. It stank everywhere of sand, concrete, and wet air.

Despite everything, Helmut thought they were well-positioned; the Flakvierling stood secure and the estuary pointed to the sea. Ammunition was sufficient. The cannon gave Helmut and the loading helpers confidence.

Now, in the dark, the cannon seemed almost eerie; the pipes shone wet, but everything was ready to go. Helmut grabbed his assault rifle. Cold metal, like murder... or suicide, if you like. It was self-defense against soldiers landing soldiers by sea or air and attacks coming from soldiers already on the ground. He picked up the rifle and scanned the horizon with the target grain. There, in the distance above the water, hardly recognizable in the darkness, a black dot seemed to move up and down. Helmut put down the rifle again and walked half-nervously to the neighboring pillow-box, where his colleagues in the Coast Guard had entrenched themselves with their MG-42.

"Hey, do you have more coffee?"

"Sure, so long as stocks last."

Great guy, the MG gunman, thought Helmut. *A quiet, proud guy.* He could be happy with his MG-42; they had two of them in the pillow-box, and this fat black MG was brand new and respectfully dangerous, a world apart from the old Model 34.

Helmut could see clearly now; these men of the bunker crew were armed with the most modern weapons, including MP44s for close combat. They also had a couple of Panzerschreck weapons, in addition to the more short-range Panzerfausts. *It should be possible to defend the bunker if it comes to it.*

"Shit, let us sleep," swore a soldier lying on the ground. Helmut served himself from the pot, went outside, and walked the few meters back to the Flakvierling, his eyes on the dark sea. Earlier, he had clearly seen something blinking there.

Soon, the night would finally be over, but somehow, sleep was out of the question. Helmut knelt on one leg and pressed his hand into the sand. He picked up a lump with his fist and looked carefully as the grains trickled between his fingers. *If it starts, you have to get out unhurt*, he told himself.

Helmut got up and looked at the rough, dark sea. *I have to get away from this bastard of a situation, in this dirty little corner of the world.* It was a strange thought, right here and now. *But is it better anywhere else? Not in this war.* Hamburg, where he still thought of as home, had been flattened by the English. This was no war against soldiers, only bombers against civilians. Cowards. Terrorists, one should probably say.

What the hell, the army is too staid for me, and after my little missteps in my 1940 affair with the daughter of a colonel, I was back on the street. Just like my mother. Actually, he should not feel anything, but his thoughts wandered. *True, I did not have a father, but when I was a small child, he had fled to America, fled from the Nazis. At least, that's what my mother said.* Helmut smirked in irony. *But now, the Flak Unit is my home. We are real comrades, and we won't let anyone take the piss out of us.*

The tiredness drove him to his knees. He flinched, and soon, sleep would catch up with him. He thought of Nicole, the beguiling little Frenchwoman. *Madness.* A short time ago, she had almost put him on the block, intentionally or not. It was not so long ago when they drove together with their buddies through the Bocage, the green hedgerow landscapes that ran from the coast through the whole of Normandy...

Memories became a dream.

Looking out at the rolling fields of the Normandy countryside, their patchwork of colors in shades of green—moss and olive, lime and sage—it was easy to forget about the war. Trees still grew in the forests, untouched by the ravages of man. Birds still swooped from branch to branch, and on the horizon, sunlight still sparkled on the sea.

Helmut took a deep breath, gripping the wheel of the Kuebelwagen he was navigating through this green landscape of fields and brushes, so different from Hamburg and all the photographs he'd seen of how the war had taken its toll on other places around Europe and beyond. Bombed-out shells of cities, the gray, smoke-filled skies, the slashes of scarlet on comrades long gone… He was thankful that these were not the views that faced him in Normandy. That day, he was also thankful to have the chance to take his friends for a drive. Strictly speaking, he wasn't supposed to be using the Wehrmacht's car today. Military transport vehicles were prohibited for non-essential tasks, mainly due to the petrol shortage. But going for a scenic country drive with his two best comrades and three pretty French girls they'd picked up didn't exactly count as essential, and Helmut knew it. But he dared to take the vehicle anyway, crammed it full of friends, and drove out into the spring afternoon.

They'd been in a jovial mood, he and his buddies from the Flak Unit, after making a good trade earlier in the day: French cognac for tobacco. It was quite a deal, and there was tons of it. And maybe it was this little streak of luck that had given him this jubilant attitude and had prompted him to take the Kuebelwagen. Trade was a risky business, however—for both sides. The local civilians bartered their bread and liquor, trading for items such as pottery and cigarettes. Despite the frequent trades he witnessed and took part in, there was a lot of mistrust between the parties and he knew one had to be extra careful. You never could tell who was being honest and who might be part of the resistance.

But that French girl was an exception, or almost. Nicole was a redhead with springy, curling locks and eyes as green as an emerald—but his attachment to her was skin-deep, at best. He never got close to anyone, least of all a foreign girl.

Just a few days ago, he had pulled up at an opening to an empty field, their view of the sea unfettered. Only a short drive out of the city, and it was like the war was a distant memory.

As Nicole stepped down from the back of the car, it was her long, smooth legs that were occupying Helmut's thoughts. He knew the reasons why attractive French girls were so keen to hook up with German officers such as himself. That's why he found it easy to stay unattached to his girlfriends—they had agendas too. For starters, if they so happened to be secret members of the resistance, they would gain valuable information by dating someone like him. Even if their intentions had nothing to do with spying, it was undeniable that a French girl could find herself better off by dating a German. There were certain perks that local boys couldn't offer, such as being able to pay with coins and currency. Although many of the young officers were married, they were a long way from home, and it had been a long time since they'd seen their wives. So, stepping out with pretty French girls had benefits for them too.

Nicole wasn't as brash as some of the other girls Helmut had encountered. She wasn't over the top, didn't laugh as loud as the others, or make such hasty decisions. She was quieter, mysterious, the kind of girl he liked better than those brazen women that his comrades usually chased after.

The girls were talking about their alleged suffering, having no work, no trade, their sick grandmothers, and God knew what else. But there was trade everywhere - with Germans. Most of the locals relied on the Germans for trade, and young girls did trade quite a lot. It was often the same old game of flesh for money, goods, and favors.

But that girl, Nicole, was different. For a time, it felt like sincerity, but then, it all changed…and besides, she had a family—that much he knew about her—and and girls like her could easily be accused of collaboration. Why was he drawn to her like a moth to a candle? In his mind, Helmut could now clearly see her face up close, almost as if their faces would touch each other. And then he saw faces of men, French civilians and their weapons. And then, there was darkness.

Helmut winced, and suddenly, he was awake. He picked himself up. Something forced him up. Tiredness gave way to creeping nervousness. He reached for the binoculars. There, on the horizon on the sea, something flashed in the deep gray darkness. Or so he thought.

Like a ghost, the lights were gone again. He shook his head. He was having a restless night, so real sleep was out of the question. He had to grin to himself. *Another night in this shithole.* Just dirt; around him lay lop-sided, half-dozing soldiers, wrapped in old blankets and coats, snoring and coughing. They were his unit, and behind him was a bunker with limited durability and lifespan.

"Fresh soup?" asked the croaking voice of a veteran soldier from whose neck dangled a dusty Iron Cross.

"You mean breakfast today is the dirty, watered down broth from yesterday, don't you?" But Helmut did not really care.

The comrade nodded resignedly. "Most importantly, it's something warm; it is pretty cold tonight."

"And we are at the start of June, summertime for the Atlantic."

"Time to wake up," he thought out loud, ignoring the insignificant remark of a comrade lying on the floor.

Helmut walked back to the Flakvierling. Here, he was in charge. He was the gunner. Helmut's comrade and buddy, one of the loaders, Herbert, had already smoked his third cigarette of the morning. Again and again, he looked nervously at the wristwatch. "Helmut, what do you think the day will bring?"

Helmut shrugged his shoulders. "I just hope it won't be like the last few days. As you know, there were increased bomb attacks everywhere in Normandy. I'm telling you, something big is in the air."

"There have been bomb attacks before" Herbert argued.

Helmut nodded in silence and then, looked through the binoculars into the gray night sky that was nearing its end.

Herbert was bobbing his heels up and down. "Good luck comes from above."

Helmut could barely hide his tension. "Further north, the bombers blew everything down yesterday. Several hundred men were killed."

Herbert nodded, looking concerned. "I've been in some serious battles too. I was stationed in the Reich as a flak helper. The heavy Liberator bombers came every few days - hundreds, one immense formation after the next. But all the planes flying at an altitude of 5,000 or above couldn't do much. The bombers threw their heavy one thousand pounds of suitcases on us. It was an inferno of explosions, embers, smoke, and burning debris. The civilian population was hit particularly hard. I tell you this is no longer a normal war, with death by fire and mass extinction. We have something to do here, that much I can tell you."

"Try to stay calm, Herbert. You'll make everyone nervous."

Helmut held up the binoculars again and tried to peer at something in the gray semi-darkness of the ocean. Was there something blinking again? Nothing. He shook his head, pulled a cigarette out of his jacket, and leaned against a sandbag. He looked back at the last few days.

Would they come today? And if they did, would he survive today? Inwardly, he nodded complacently. Despite everything, he had always come through well. He could not credit himself, as a flak soldier low-flying aircraft had almost destroyed him a couple of times. There was also the time before Leningrad and the Eastern Front. Helmut jerked out another cigarette. In the last few weeks, he had actually become a smoker. Everything was about the nerves, and, they were hardly ever reading blank. The tension of his comrades was contagious. Most veterans smelled of it. In addition, there were the supply difficulties, and, of course, the drama with Nicole. *Just don't think about her again.*

Somewhere in the distance, aircraft engines hummed, but they did not seem to approach, rather disappearing to the east, but still looking for their targets here near the Normandy coast. The increasingly frequent flying formations did not fly towards the Reich; everyone had noticed that by now. The comrades sensed that these occurrences were no coincidence, as the signs thickened daily. Since the latter part of May 1944, the enemy air forces had been attacking combat installations and position-finding equipment along the coast as far as he could see and gather but without any apparent point of concentration.

Helmut was sure that it was about to begin. The Anglo-Saxons would try it very soon. That much was clear. *Would they come here, though, directly to Normandy?* Rommel had a good reputation. *If they land directly on the Normandy coast,. Rommel will get us out of trouble.*

Something was humming in the sky, deep and close. It was aircraft propellers again, but the sound was different; these were not bombers. *Transport aircraft? Here above these waters?* The droning was damn near. "Do you hear that? Airplanes, but no bombers."

"Maybe our Luftwaffe?" rasped the old soldier.

Helmut scanned the horizon and then, looked back at the sea. He started. Again, he put on the binoculars. Something was blinking on the horizon again, several times, for sure. "Hey, wake up the other loaders as a precaution, and get the staff officer; something's not right here."

Disgruntled, Herbert sauntered off, mumbling, "... but not today ... right?"

The Atlantic Wall - Early Spring 1944

The road became narrower until it consisted of only gravel and dune sand. Slowly, the Horch limousine passed an unfinished bunker as tall as a skyscraper. Field Marshal Rommel felt slightly annoyed, but he could not pay any attention to personal comfort. Duty came first, and everything else was secondary.

The driver, Lang, did his best to at least avoid the coarsest potholes. Several dozen soldiers were apparently deployed as active construction workers, building the bunker. Colonel-General Speidel was accompanying his superior on this "excursion," which he called the inspection trip, to the Atlantic coast. Speidel shook his head in disbelief.

The Field Marshal was surprised, too. "What do you think, Speidel? If the men have to work all day, would they be able to fight if the enemy were to land tonight?"

"I hope so. But what can we do? The bunkers have to be finished."

"Well, if they're going to get finished, let's hope it'll be soon." The Field Marshal cast a concerned look out the window. "Do you see this large arch on the bunker, Speidel?"

"You mean the large concrete dome, Herr Field Marshal?"

"That will be an artillery bunker platform."

Field Marshal Rommel beckoned Lang to slow down so that he could take a closer look at the gigantic monument and hill site.

"See, Speidel, these are supposed to be the bulwarks of our Atlantic Wall, equipped with big guns. And with a bit of imagination, maybe one day, something will become of it."

"Yes, I hope that with the help of those guns, we'll beat the enemy back."

"Me too. And I'll tell you one more thing, Speidel: directly on the beach, regardless of whether it's here in Normandy or somewhere else, the war will be won or lost on the coast. The first 48 hours of the invasion will be decisive. For both the Allies and for Germany, it will be the longest day."

"We need to stay optimistic, Herr Field Marshal."

Rommel could not suppress an ironic smile. "I wish I had your optimism, Speidel, but this concrete pile next to us is supposed to one day become the mighty, heavy seaside quay Albert, only it was scheduled for completion five months ago. You understand?"

"Of course; it's taking too long. Drive on, Lang."

Lang simply nodded and sped up again. He could palpably feel the frustrations of the General and those of the long-serving Field Marshal.

"And do you think, Speidel, that this whole bunker construction makes any sense?"

"When they're finished, they'll be formidable facilities. They'll be equipped with heavy artillery. It'll give the enemy something to nibble on."

Rommel pressed his lips together. "Do you really believe that? What do you think the heavy artillery can do?"

"Capture naval targets and disable even heavy ships, including battleships and cruisers."

"Correct, heavy naval targets. And what do you think will land here first?"

"Well, I would say assault boats."

"Exactly. And the heavy guns will have to fire on all of them?"

"Well, that depends how large they are, and their speed. Theoretically, that is already possible. And when they have been hit the first time….."

Rommel shook his head. "It's all so wrong. The armada that lands will consist of thousands of ships. Five thousand, maybe 7,000. Hundreds of landing craft, one wave after the next. I'm telling you I don't worry much about heavy ship guns and long loading times."

"The navy sees it differently though. And as far as I know, so does the leadership."

"The leadership. All dilettantes. I say they all have no clue."

"Field Marshal, von Rundstedt is one of the longest-serving and most respected Field Marshals of the Reich. I think he knows what he's talking about."

"He should, Speidel, he should. But neither he, nor the Organisation Todt have an inkling of what we have to deal with. This is not the enemy of 1940. In Italy, we already began to see what the enemy is capable of." Rommel shook his head in disbelief. "The bunkers aren't enough to defend against an invasion. The enemy will come with an armada of landers of all sizes, airborne troops, and an air fleet unlike the world has ever seen. The truth is that I have to come up with something."

"You mean a different strategy than the one previously laid out?"

"That's what it looks like to me. I have to come up with something, possibly against the dictates of the leadership. Because one thing's for sure: we have no chance with what we have!"

"Maybe you should talk with von Rundstedt."

"I'll see all the people in charge at the next briefing in Berchtesgaden. Until then, I need to have an alternative plan finalized."

"But I have to ask you directly, Herr Field Marshal," began Speidel, "you have freedom of action, right? I mean, you can do what you want here, or not."

With a somewhat artificial grin, the Field Marshal turned to the Colonel-General. "I wish it were like that. You can see for yourself how fast this is going on, especially with the heavy bunkers. It doesn't mean anything anyway, I tell you. I'm just a kind of flagship general for the propaganda, and probably to keep the troops happy."

"What do you think we should do if this goes wrong? We have to play politics, right?"

Rommel rubbed and pulled at his nose. "Good question, Speidel. I know that you and your friends like dealing with politics, and I know you are preparing something. Be very careful and keep me out of it. I'll hold myself back from politics for now. First, we have to strike back against the Anglo-Americans. Then, we'll see. Do you understand, Speidel?"

"Yes. I only hope they don't come this summer"

"They're coming, Speidel. I know only one real enemy now, and that's time."

Speidel crossed his arms and nodded.

"Lang," Rommel said as he tapped his driver on the shoulder, "drive over to the right. Look over there, Speidel. There is a flak cannon and unit over there. And the boys look fresh. Let's take a look."

"Very good," added Speidel. "Flak Units of the Luftwaffe. A lot depends on them."

Lang could see from the Horch limousine that the Field Marshal was not only a quick thinker but also a physically active initiator. *The Field Marshal is right,* thought Lang. The Organisation Todt was really useless, even less so the responsible Inspector of the Fortifications; then, the construction work was carried on uniformly through the Inspector of the Engineers and Fortresses and with the aid of Organisation Todt. And according to Rommel, the work was strongly influenced and personally supervised by the Fuehrer himself, who had commissioned him with the completion of the Atlantic Wall, and yet the command authority lay in other hands.

Our Flak Unit

"We swapped the cognac for cigarettes" said the young soldier as he sat down on the hood of the bucket car.

Helmut nodded. Spread out in front of him were boxes of provisions and wine and spirit bottles. "How many boxes of cognac did you bring?" A loader carried a box over his shoulder. "This morning, there were six more. We finished half, so best wishes for your birthday!"

"Thanks, comrades," said Helmut. "Cheers, to us. Break a leg!" Helmut could feel the effect of the French luxury liquor. He felt cheered, but somehow, drained at the same time. He preferred to rest. Birthday parties were not his thing, but how could he refuse them? It seemed that one or other of the comrades of the Flak Unit always were always having a birthday, and since they were not fighting, there was also plenty of time to kill.

"You look awful, birthday boy" grumbled the young loader from behind Helmut. "I bet you've drank the contents of all these empty bottles yourself."

Helmut pulled a small soldier's pocket mirror out of his jacket. "You're right, I look better than you all" he replied mockingly; in fact, Helmut did not like what he saw in the mirror. Despite the half-darkness in the shadow of the large concrete bunker, he was startled by his neglected appearance. His dark hair lay low over his forehead and his cheeks seemed more pronounced, probably the result of the Wehrmacht diet, which in recent weeks consisted of thin pea soup and exchanged bread with the natives. His stubblebeard could have passed him off smoothly as a submarine sailor. "You have to take this shit with humor" he stammered in soliloquy.

His comrade jabbed his elbow gently into his side. "We all look good enough, and we from the Flak never need to hide!"

"I'm not hiding from anyone" replied Helmut briskly. Gradually, Helmut felt he had enough of this birthday party, the mindless revelry and gossip.

"And what about that one up there? Do you not have to hide from him?" the comrade continued blustering.

"You mean the Fuehrer? Frankly, I'm the least interested in him, the fat Goering, and the whole brown gang, understood?"

"Hey, Helmut, don't become so quick-tempered now," the comrade said as he opened another bottle of cognac. "The times have changed. Besides, be careful with what you say. Such remarks count as degradation."

"You don't have to tell me, mate. I am still a German soldier. I fight for honor and my country."

"Yes, yes, we all say that too. Tell us, Helmut, how did you end up with the Flak?"

"Old story, but all right, I'll tell you. In the summer of '41, I knew that I would be drafted soon. It was clear that I would have landed somewhere on the Russian front. So, I volunteered for the Luftwaffe. And they sent me to the mobile Flak."

"Well done, Helmut."

"Right from the start, we were a real Flak division, and we had been split up a bit, just between infantry regiments and coastal crews. All in all, our department was densely positioned all the way to the coast. Perhaps too close, too far forward, as our old-timers - what we called the experienced soldiers, former East Front fighters - noticed, because then, lateral shifts to the East and West became so impossible. Through leadership chaos and confused orders and interference, our corps was virtually divided. Some regiments were actually deployed away from the division."

"Similar story to most of us. Yet, the Luftwaffe has always been more attractive than the stupid army."

"Be careful with your comments yourself," said Helmut.

"Here, take another sip, Helmut. And stay relaxed; it's your birthday."

"I've had enough for today. Have fun drinking. I'll put my feet up." Helmut was angry. Did the boy have to remind him today of the Fuehrer? Helmut stood in front of the bunker wall and pulled out a cigarette. He had to grin over his own thoughts. *That part about honor and country, yes, that somehow was true. But when the enemy actually lands here, hard times are ahead. And I want to survive and then, just get out of here.* Helmut shook his head. Maybe there was still a chance that he could see the small French girl, Nicole, again. *But perhaps not, because if she was part of the Resistance...* Suddenly, Helmut felt the need for a fresh drink. Thinking of Nicole had put him in a bad mood, and he did not want to be in a bad mood today.

"The birthday boy is back," said the now quite noticeably drunk comrade. "Well, the aged cognac isn't so bad, right? Where did you get it again?"

"Well, we took a trip a few days ago, me and my loaders."

The soldier grabbed the bottle and allowed himself to take a deep swig. "A tour? I thought we could get an alarm here any day?"

Unexpectedly, Helmut had to grin. "We simply organized a nice evening without bureaucracy. No one noticed. Anyway, we had some girls on board. The Kuebelwagen was full of young French girls, some even with good connections. It was really nice."

"You traded? Cognac for what?"

"Cigarettes and a bit of Wehrmacht ceramics."

"For a box of cognac?"

"Yes, and a few more boxes, and as a bonus, that one lady invited me into a vacant barn."

"If only the Fuehrer knew!"

Helmut had to laugh. "Drink up, on Fuehrer's orders! Anyway, these are probably the last boxes of cognac."

"What do you mean?" the elderly soldier demanded to know.

"Well, a couple of days ago, we thought we had finished a trade for cognac and cigarettes, but then, one box fell off the car. It broke, and there was glass everywhere."

"And all the good stuff spilled out on the street?"

"You would think that, but there were bottles with sand inside. The Frenchman who gave it to us had stuffed some of the black bottles with sand. He didn't think we would find out until it was too late for us to do anything about it."

"Too late?"

"The Allies are coming. The man figured the attack would come soon and that he wouldn't have to answer for cheating us."

"So you let it slide?"

Helmut shook his head. "Herbert, why don't you tell them?"

"Well, we went back to the garage and there he was, the elderly Frenchman we had done business with."

"And?"

"We took him for a ride. He admitted to everything."

The old soldier smirked. "I can imagine. So, then he told you guys where all the booze was hidden?"

"Yeah, that's pretty much what happened."

"But next time, we have to go fishing for booze in another village," Helmut said with a slight smirk on his face. "We can't go back there; the civilians won't trade with us anymore."

"You mean you punished the French guy?"

"It wasn't us," Herbert said. "We asked the German military police for a favor, and they were happy to oblige. They treated the old man like he was part of the Resistance."

"Hung him on a lamp post?"

"Sure, what else?" Herbert opened another bottle. "Just like all the French riff-raff deserves. Cheers, gentlemen."

"We're a colorful bunch already. Now, here we are standing on the shore, drinking and killing time."

"But our main mission remains," Helmut said seriously, "which is anti-aircraft defense. But the Army on the coast here is supposed to be aided in its ground combat as much as possible."

"Sure, if the Allies ever come around here."

Helmut remained on point. "And also against landing boats; otherwise, we wouldn't be stationed here."

The youngest comrade opened a new bottle. "I tell you one thing; buddy: we haven't been shipped here for nothing. The enemy will come very soon."

Helmut nodded in agreement. "And we seem to be starting to get a few more men, though the corps is still near Paris."

A very young bunker soldier with his helmet resting low on his forehead patted the gun barrel. "Helmut, as a rookie, I have to ask, did you always have this beautiful Flakvierling?"

"No, they're relatively new, and we have too few of them. If something happens tomorrow, we might not have enough of them; and when I say we, I mean the whole section here."

The loader interjected. "The Flakvierling is not bad, but it wasn't always this easy. Before, we had more to do with the proven 3.7, which always had to be pulled by heavy army tractors and was relatively difficult to relocate."

"I can tell you something about the Flak too" a corporal intervened. "I was in Africa, and, in between, was stationed briefly in the Reich, helped my colleagues with the batteries with 8.8 cm and 10.5 cm Flak for bombers I had as well, but for the last time for missions in North Africa. And now, the first ones arrive here. We're going to need many more before the enemy lands.

"If they come," replied the loader.

"I can confirm that with the delays, but most of the time, I've always been part of a team for this beauty here," Helmut said, pointing to the Flakvierling. "With this lightweight 20mm Flak 38, we would be able to defend against aircraft, but it can also tackle lightly armored vehicles and infantry.

The corporal also made use of the cognac box. "This thing is labor-intensive; it needs to be reloaded all the time, right?"

"You are right, and for every barrel, we need at least one loader. Six men or more. My favorite cannon is still the 20mm Vierling on half-track, the Opel Blitz. Thanks to the troops, wherever we fire, the grass will have a hard time growing."

"Hey, guys," the comrade said, pointing at the dark limousine slowly approaching the group.

"Put away the bottles!" bellowed Helmut. "We're getting visitors. Put away the bottles and pretend to be busy."

Slowly, the Horch limousine approached, stopping in front of the group of soldiers dragging boxes. This was some important group that seemed interested in Helmut's surroundings. They were here to snoop around, as Helmut and his comrades called such visits.

It looked as if senior officials were planning something at his section.

A high-ranking general and his lieutenant stepped out first, ignoring the Flak Unit's soldiers, and headed straight for the beach.

Another lean man in a dark officer's jacket and high helmet (which Helmut also recognized as a high General) and his driver slowly approached the amazed soldier.

The high officer started talking. "Stay calm, gentlemen. Even a high-ranking officer and his Field Marshal has to look to see if everything is okay."

Helmut and the soldiers put their hands to their foreheads and tapped their heels together. "Yes, Herr Colonel."

"Colonel-General, if you don't mind. Well, gentlemen, these boxes here don't look like ammunition boxes. What do we have here?"

"The truth is, there are cognac bottles in there."

"Carousing here? Are you not on duty?"

Helmut straightened his back, his hands close to his body. "Yes, Herr Colonel-General! The boxes are still unopened."

Colonel-General Speidel raised his fists to his sides "Stop it. You can't fool me!"

"Yes, sir. At your command."

The Colonel-General pointed his thumb at the big machine. "You're a Flak Unit, Luftwaffe. Tell me, what do you think of the equipment?"

"The new Flak are great, especially when they're mobile."

"Young man, you seem to have confidence in our guns."

Helmut nodded, smiling. "A Flakvierling is good for almost anything."

The Colonel-General smiled. "Especially if brand new."

"I'm sure the Luftwaffe is doing what it can."

Speidel stepped toward the Flak, visually inspected it, putting his hand on the gun barrel. "You know what, if we get enough of them, you'll all become heroes."

Helmut felt something like recognition: "It's a very good gun, deployable against ships, infantry, and aircraft, Herr Colonel-General."

He approached Helmut. "How long have you been with the Flak?"

"Since '41, Herr General."

"Very good. That means you are familiar with it."

"Only what concerns cannons and shooting."

"Well, then, the Atlantic Wall will hold, don't you agree?"

"Certainly, we will hold here."

Berchtesgaden Spring 1944

With a slightly crouched posture, his hands behind his back, the Fuehrer of the Greater German Reich entered the reception hall. When he appeared, everyone immediately fell silent.

"One hundred men and one order," old Field Marshal von Rundstedt whispered humorously to his old friend and companion Field Marshal von Kluge. The latter only cleared his throat; for in all the crowds and talk there were probably 50 men in the room—from old-fashioned Marshals to staff helpers to SS servants serving cognac and coffee; just about everyone of rank and name in the Wehrmacht was there.

The Fuehrer began to speak. "In the room shall remain Jodl, von Schweppenburg, the Field Marshals von Rundstedt, von Kluge, and Rommel, as well as Herr Guderian. You stay as well." The Fuehrer nodded to his old friend and companion, Sepp Dietrich.

All the men moved a few steps backwards and then, stood in a closed row in front of the Fuehrer. They were as silent as students awaiting a scolding from the teacher. They were Field Marshal von Rundstedt, the Commander-in-Chief West; General Field Marshal von Kluge, Field Marshal and Commander of the Atlantic Wall; Rommel; the Commander-in-Chief in Italy, Kesselring, Colonel-General Guderian; and General of the Panzer Troop West, General von Schweppenburg, Colonel-General of the Waffen SS; and Fuehrer of the 1st Panzer Army, Sepp Dietrich.

To the side and behind the Field Marshals were SS guards, their hands behind their backs, but with their pistols locked and loaded and within reach. Unobtrusively, in the corner, was Field Marshal von Kluge who looked nervously at his wristwatch every few minutes. Opposite the map table stood the Fuehrer of the German Reich, pounding with both hands on the map and looking icily around at the officers. "Gentlemen, as you know, we must now doubt that the enemy, as previously assumed, wants to land at the narrowest part of the channel. There will probably be an accompanying invasion as well. They have possibilities almost everywhere. Maybe as far away as the Balkans". The Fuehrer pointed to the place card with a pencil, "But they'll probably land here, in the south of France."

"My Fuehrer" interjected Rommel. "If I may remark, the enemy does not have to land on Par De Calais; they have possibilities further south. East of the Somme, Normandy, or, rather, from the very south."

The Fuehrer looked at him coldly. "Yes, but I would ask you not to interrupt me... And now, gentlemen, what do you think, where will they try? May I first ask you, Herr von Rundstedt?"

"Of course," the old Field Marshal strode forward from the line and pointed at the map. "Well, I'm sure they will land at the very narrowest part of the channel at Calais."

"What makes you so sure?" the Fuehrer interjected.

"Well, first of all, an attack from Dover on Calais would be the shortest sea route across to the continent. Second, our V1 and most of all the V2, which I assume will soon be available for deployment and, of which the enemy also knows, are all up there at Calais. Third, this is the shortest route to the Ruhr and the industrial heart of Germany. If the enemy lands there on the channel, he would reach the Rhine in just four days."

The Fuehrer turned to von Kluge. "Field Marshal, you have the floor."

"As we all know, we made an extensive planning exercise with many experts and involving all branches of the Wehrmacht. This exercise took place in Paris in the middle of February 1944. The conclusions drawn from this exercise pointed to the mouth of the Rhone, the Cotentin peninsula, and the Channel coast between Ostend and the Somme as the most endangered areas. Because of the large tonnage of the Allied fleet and the great number of available divisions, the possibility of an invasion near the mouth of the Loire should also not be disregarded."

The Fuehrer nodded thoughtfully. "Now to you, Herr Rommel; where do you think?"

Rommel nodded, pointing with a wooden ruler. "Here would be a logical possibility." The ruler pointed to the narrowest point between Britain and the continent. "But more likely is Normandy, including Cotentin. The peninsula, as well as the wide beach, offers excellent possibilities to establish a bridgehead with a broad front."

The Fuehrer bent low over the map and looked up at Rommel. "How do you think the enemy will act?"

"First, they will bombard our positions, then send attack-boats and landing craft."

Rommel moved closer to the map of Europe, signaling with a generous wave of his hand. "Then, under the cover of artillery and bombers, airborne troops will be placed behind the front."

Von Rundstedt cleared his throat and stopped. "So, as the Supreme Commander West. I have to ask you, Herr Rommel, what would be your counter move?"

Rommel raised his voice slightly. "The enemy will be killed at the landing. The beach is the battle line!"

"That's empty talk, Herr Rommel." Von Schweppenburg pointed his hand along the coastline from Holland to the Spanish border. "How can you defend an over 2,000km coastline? We don't have the forces for that!"

Rommel folded his hands behind his back. "We'll send all armored divisions to the coast. I'll show you." Rommel moved to the miniature battlefield; a gigantic sandbox full of various small wooden blocks that represented bunkers, panzers, and divisions. "Let me show it to you right here. As shown here, it will be the same all over the Atlantic Wall."

The Fuehrer followed, and with narrowed eyes bent low over the sandpit, following Rommel's forefinger and hints.

"We do not need big bunkers and fortifications," Rommel said. "Instead, we focus our efforts on alternatives."

Von Rundstedt interrupted in a low voice. "But, Herr Rommel, we need big bunkers with artillery to make it more difficult for the enemy to penetrate the hinterland as the artillery fires at the ships."

"Gentlemen," Rommel continued, "obstacles placed in front of the beach make it harder to land enemy landing ships, and our batteries, guns, and small arms will attack the first landing phase. And where they are not available, our strong panzer force shall take over that task."

The Fuehrer approached the sandbox and pointed to the gaps between the bunkers. "There will always be a few gaps. What equipment do you intend to prioritize deploying?"

"I suggest placing massive anti-aircraft cannons, mainly small and medium caliber, directly at the front behind the beach. In addition, we'll make massive use of heavy MGs with all resistance points placed close to each other, especially in Normandy. And as I said, we can use the panzers at the front."

As if suddenly stung, von Schweppenburg interrupted. "If the enemy manages to break through at only one point of the defense line suggested by the Herr Field Marshal, then the Reich will be completely at the mercy of enemy troops. The Anglo-Americans could march straight to Germany, all the way to Berlin, and our panzers can only follow them!"

Guderian stepped forward: "Our panzers will have captured and annihilated the enemy at every conceivable landing site within 48 hours."

Gesturing, Rommel lightly beat his fist on the table. "Your panzers are nowhere! Before their panzers even come close to the coast, the enemy air force will have bombed all the panzers and troops to lumps and ashes!"

Rommel turned to the Fuehrer. "My Fuehrer... I ask you to subordinate the Panzer Group to my command. This is the only way we can prevent the enemy's impending invasion."

The Fuehrer stared silently, iron-faced.

Von Rundstedt immediately took the floor. "But then, we'd be betting everything on one card. We would have no strategic reserves at all. As Commander-in-Chief West, I cannot be responsible for that."

The Fuehrer shook his head in disgust. "Well, von Rundstedt, for three years, you have allowed the Atlantic Wall to be inadequate, while Herr Rommel in the shortest period of time has done exemplary work. An invasion must be prevented under all circumstances. And one thing is undeniable. After a failed landing, the enemy will not try a second time." The Fuehrer strode to a large map of Europe. "Then, we will finally have the forces that we so desperately need in the East. A whole 45 divisions!" Slowly, the Fuehrer approached Field Marshal Rommel. "On you... and your soldiers depends the outcome of the war. And with it the fate of the Reich and of the whole nation. Are you aware of this, Field Marshal?"

"Yes, my Fuehrer."

The Fuehrer sat down and wiped his forehead with a handkerchief.

For a few moments, no one dared speak.

"My Fuehrer," Von Rundstedt ventured, raising his visibly reddened head, "I have to ask you. We also need to talk about where the landing is most likely. Because we only know that the enemy is coming, not where and not when. Look at the map here." The old Field Marshal pointed at the red blocks on the British Channel, the narrowest point between the British Isles and the Continent.

"We have to assume that the enemy would come where it can lead to the fastest success. We can assume they will try it here on the canal just north of Calais."

"Jodl, please," interrupted the Fuehrer dryly.

The Chief of the Wehrmacht Operations Staff picked up his coat and walked up to the group with his chin up standing directly next to the Fuehrer. "We have not believed in that for some time. The

Military Command is now convinced, in the meantime, that the allegedly sighted armored units around and behind Dover are a decoy operation, a deception. The English want to fool us here."

The Fuehrer looked to Guderian. "Herr Guderian, do you think we could do as Field Marshal Rommel says?"

Colonel-General Guderian, the Inspector of the Panzer Forces, also took three steps forward, standing next to Rommel. "No, I do not, my Fuehrer." Then, he turned to Rommel. "Herr Rommel, the panzer division will remain in the hinterland, not on the coast. That will not work. I have to say that directly to you."

"Excuse me, but you do not have to tell me anything," Rommel replied briskly. "My Fuehrer," Rommel spoke again, "it's imperative that with my plan, we beat the enemy right on the beach."

Guderian shook his head, smiling. "You want to use Panzerschreck against landing Shermans and Churchills? And to embed our strongest weapon, mobile panzers? What do you think will happen?" Guderian turned to Hitler. "My Fuehrer, Herr Rommel's plan is madness. It will not go well. He will not get any panzers from me for such nonsense."

"Herr von Schweppenburg," said the Fuehrer, "you, as Commander of the Panzer Troops West, how would you proceed?"

"Let me first see my Fuehrer" said von Schweppenburg. "In view of the formidable enemy's air superiority and the number, caliber, and effectiveness of the naval guns of the combined Anglo-American battle fleets, we can't prevent them landing some place on nearly 2,000 km of coastline, and I am certain that they would succeed in any case. The only solution would be to utilize the only German superiority—that of a strategic mobile reserves. High-quality panzer units should be held in reserve to crush an enemy penetration inland. We beat the enemy with our armored troops, divide them up, surround them, and destroy them."

The Fuehrer straightened his glasses. "Herr Rommel, again to you. You said you want to repel the enemy on the coast. What's missing up front to prevent you from doing it?"

"To be able to defend right up front, I would need more troops, and I would need hundreds of light flak, and the infantry would need the new STG-44 assault rifle. Apart from that, complete equipment with the new MG-42. We need anti-aircraft towers. Small, narrow, maybe 10-meter-high concrete towers, a tower at least every 200 meters a tower. And of course, panzers."

"Do you also want to put panzers on your towers?" Guderian added ironically.

"By no means. We are setting up the Eighty-eight there. They can be used against heavy landing craft, light warships, and, of course, as permanent protection against aircraft, which we expect in the hundreds.

The Fuehrer nodded in agreement. "You are against setting up a bunker system?"

"They will not be finished in time. And small weapons will decide the battle, gentlemen. Big bunkers and heavy anti-ship guns are too inflexible. They're part of an old, worn out strategy that I reject."

Von Schweppenburg waved his hand condescendingly. "And you would try to succeed with all those trivial defenses on the beach? That won't work. The enemy has an armada of at least 4,000 ships. They will break through somewhere. You can't prevent that."

Rommel sighted. "On the contrary, we can defeat the enemy up front."

Von Rundstedt cleared his throat. "Herr Rommel, we do not have as much material as you need. And the enemy still has enough power to attack us in several places at the same time." Von Rundstedt walked slowly over to the large map and pointed to the center of France. "Here, in the center, I will assemble my force for a counterstrike, no matter where the enemy lands. A mighty panzer army that I can maneuver in any direction, along with concentrated air attacks, so I can cut off the landed enemy from the coast. Russia has shown us that flexible defense with panzers, if applied correctly, is the best strategy."

Guderian nodded, standing next to the Fuehrer and pointing to the map.

"Field Marshal von Rundstedt is right. The German panzer forces are one of the few arms that are superior to that of the Allies. Our panzers beat the enemy panzers, no doubt. A flexible, heavily concentrated panzer army will chase the Anglo-Saxons back into the sea, no matter where they land. By the channel or in southern France, we need a central panzer army."

Rommel stomped nervously up and down the hall. "That's not right," interrupted the Field Marshal impetuously. "The Anglo-Saxons have such huge air forces that they can destroy entire divisions from the air alone! We won't be able to move, not even at night!"

"Herr Rommel," interrupted Hitler. "You have to realize that we need reserves. We need the panzers to make counterstrikes. And also, the issue with the bunkers is a proven concept that you have to accept. Of course, they have to be completed as soon as possible."

"My Fuehrer," Rommel said as he took a deep breath, "I need the panzers at the front. I ask you to leave all available panzers to me."

"Then, you'll make every sideways shift impossible," interrupted Guderian loudly.

The Fuehrer rose. "All in all, I agree with Rommel that the enemy cannot be permitted to land. But with the bunkers and small arms, and especially with the panzers, we will still have to see. Well, thank you for your interpretations. I will respond to your suggestions. We are finished for now."

"One more thing, my Fuehrer," Rommel interjected.

"What is it Herr Rommel?"

"My Fuehrer, when we're done with it—I mean, if the landing fails—they will not come back for a long time. Then, there will be a completely new political situation for us."

"What do you mean by that, please?"

"Well, my Fuehrer, after we have repelled the Anglo-Saxons, we will be in a different political situation. That is, we can bargain with the Western powers from a position of strength. Besides, we would be …"

"What are you talking about?" Sepp Dietrich questioned as he jumped up, staring at Rommel with his mouth open.

Rommel looked around. He was greeted by cold looks from the generals, showing their arrogant contempt. "Gentlemen," Rommel began.

"Field Marshal," interrupted the Fuehrer, "I have to ask you to focus solely on your military duties. Have I expressed myself clearly enough?"

"Yes, my Fuehrer!"

The Fuehrer spurned him by turning and walking away from Rommel. "We are finished now. And, once more, gentleman, every one of you would do well not to disappoint me. All of you have a great responsibility. It's all about passing or failing." With a quick gesture of his hand, the Fuehrer disappeared, while all the generals raised their arms in the German salute as a farewell.

All the men moved to leave the hall as fast as possible. Only Rommel stayed. He stared at the map. *Had they not understood anything?* The door opened again, and von Schweppenburg, the General of the Panzer troops West returned. With his hands clasped behind his back, he walked slowly towards his officially higher ranked Field Marshal. "My dear Rommel, I have to tell you something else. What you have just stated goes too far. How could you talk such nonsense? Tell me, Rommel," von Schweppenburg said as he approached to within a hand's width, "after things didn't go so well in North Africa, why didn't you retire? I admit you were a good division commander. But this is all a bit too big for you, isn't it?"

Blood shot into Rommel's face. "I forbid your brash tone. I'm still a Field Marshal!"

"Gentlemen, do not get upset. The meeting is already over." Rommel and von Schweppenburg turned around to see the veteran Field Marshal von Rundstedt, his hands behind his back, holding a Marshal's baton.

"Herr von Schweppenburg, you are absolutely right," von Rundstedt said, beckoning to his old companion half-smilingly. "Only, if we want to turn the tide again, the younger generation of Field Marshals must sometimes listen to the veterans, without wanting to insist on personal connections to the Fuehrer. You surely accept that, Herr Rommel, don't you?"

"Herr von Rundstedt," Rommel interjected angrily "I would also ask you to hold yourself back; otherwise, I'll have to complain about you."

Von Rundstedt nodded his approval to the two opponents. "Now, calm down, gentlemen. Where will this lead, if not even *we* can find common ground?"

Von Schweppenburg snorted. "Well, you try talking sense to this Swabian. I say goodbye, gentlemen." He tapped his cap and walked with large steps outside.

Von Rundstedt corrected his monocle. "My dear Herr Rommel, you have made a great impression on the Fuehrer, but do you think that will lead to anything?"

Rommel cleared his throat, tapping his heels impatiently. "With all due respect, Field Marshal, I am the one who has the most experience against the Western powers and so I came to the belief that I understand something of the opponent and his methods. Furthermore, I understand my trade like any other German Field Marshal. That, you can believe."

Von Rundstedt shook his head, and Rommel thought he could make out a slightly disconcerted smile in the wrinkles of the old Field Marshal's face.

"My dear Herr Rommel," von Rundstedt said, his tone sounding slightly presumptuous, "I'll give you a suggestion. Your headquarters are in northern France, La Roche-Guyon, aren't they?"

Rommel nodded in silence.

"Now, Herr Rommel, since I am still the Commander-in-Chief West and currently live near Paris, I suggest that you come over to have lunch with me this week. I'm sure there are some things that will interest you very much. What do you say?"

Rommel's features remained cool, but a secret, mischievous smile escaped the corner of his mouth. He raised his Marshal's baton. "Of course, Herr von Rundstedt. See you next week."

Von Rundstedt returned the salute.

A Prelude in Brighton

Elmer was sitting on a bench across the street from the casino, drinking a bottle of beer when his friend Walter arrived. A steady drizzle was falling as Walter sat down, pulled out his cigarettes, and offered Elmer one. The other man took one, and they sat with the unlit cigarettes dangling from their lips. "We should head to that bar on the other side of the barracks," Elmer said after a long stretch of silence.

"I thought we were going to the casino tonight," Walter said, unable to hide his annoyance. "We've been planning this for weeks."

"I just want to go find a girl," Elmer said. "You know how many of them broads are interested in us GIs. That bar down by the barracks leaves me enough time to spend in the company of a lady before I have to get back."

"Those girls aren't ladies," Walter said with a derisive snort. "And you're a fool if you think that they are."

The fact that Elmer didn't look hurt in the least made Walter mad. His naïve friend nodded amiably. "They're still nice to look at," he said.

"They're from the gutter," Walter said, venom dripping from his voice. "This war, us being here in England… Unless you find something that's worth doing here, it's all a huge waste of time. I don't even know if this war is worth it for America."

"Why is this war a waste of time?" Elmer asked, irritated. "It's going to be a sweet ride all the way to France."

"Sure, but why not trying to make something out of it? I mean, there's got to be something in this for us, right?"

"You are a strange fellow, you know that?" Elmer observed as he stood.

"Why do you say that?"

Ignoring the question, Elmer said, "Last time, you told me you had a brother over there in France, serving in the Wehrmacht."

"So?"

"Are you going to look for him?"

"Should I try to find him after the landing? He must have become a Nazi. God help me if I see him again before the war ends. I would question him, for sure. "

"All right. But If he were standing in front of you, with a gun pointed at you to block you from invading Nazi territory, would you shoot him?"

For a second, Walter looked sideways. "I guess so. Every active fighter is a Nazi. Brother or not, I would shoot. Yeah, you could say so."

Walter thought about his brother a few seconds longer, and the thoughts disturbed him. *Why did Elmer have to bring that up?*

Elmer took another sip from the bottle. "Could be that your brother is stationed in the back. Besides, not everybody fights. He could be a cook, you know?

"Yeah, I know, and we'll see what happens. But let's stop this nonsense talk and go over to the casino, right?"

Elmer shook his head. "I'm going to the bar. Are you coming with me or not?"

"Not," Walter replied. "I'm going to the casino like we planned."

"Suit yourself," Elmer said as he stuffed his hands into his pockets and headed off down the street.

Walter lit his cigarette and stewed over his friend's departure. He couldn't believe the nerve Elmer had. Walter had at least tried to look like a gentleman today. With his best jacket and pressed shirt, he planned to make his case, to find someone suitable and lucrative, right there in the casino.

After watching the large, middle-aged woman in an oversized black dress and Edwardian hat lose several rounds in a row, Walter approached her and said, "Would you mind if I offered you a few pointers, ma'am?"

The woman gave him a doubtful look, but nodded. Walter leaned close to her and started to whisper tricks he had learned from his own days as a fairly successful gambler. When the woman won the next round, she declared, "You must be my good luck charm. Sit here beside my daughter, Emily. I'll let you know if I need any more pointers."

Walter, delighted that his plan had worked so well, sat down next to the younger woman, Emily and gave her his most charming smile. She smiled back shyly, and he was pleased to see that she was as beautiful up close as she had seemed from across the room.

Her blue eyes shone and her blond bob curled softly around her ears and chin.

"Are you American?" the girl asked.

"I am," he said. "I'm Walter. Walter Schmidt."

"I'm Emily," the girl said.

"What are you doing here tonight, Emily?" he asked.

She rolled her eyes demurely and tipped her chin toward her mother. "She was invited to come by a very minor gentleman who runs things in this town. She thinks it will improve our social standing to be seen with him."

"And where is he now?" Walter asked. He could see that Emily's mother had good sense when it came to social class.

"Probably getting sloshed at the bar," she said.

"Hmmm," Walter commented with a frown. That didn't do him any good. He liked what he saw in this girl. She was hot and direct. He thought that being seeing with her and her mother made good sense. The two of them chatted until the older woman was done playing.

"Are you in a gambling mood?" Emily's mother asked Walter.

"Always am," he replied, bowing slightly.

She smirked and nodded. "Let's go over to the roulette table. I could need a lucky and noticing win tonight."

"Mom! "Emily jumped forward. "You gambled it all away, didn't you?"

Walter didn't want to listen, but it was still quite amusing hearing them arguing. He followed them and they were hardly seated before the mother beckoned him to make a bet and spin.

The dealer lady chuckled and shoved a stack of colored chips toward Walter. The result was a shock. Nobody, not even Walter could believe that he had won. Everybody burst out in excitement.

Emily's mother seemed proud, but then, she noticed the time.

"Oh, dear, Emily," she said, pressing her hand to her chest. "We need to hurry home before your father returns."

"I'll walk you out," Walter offered.

Emily took his right arm, and her mother took his left. The three of them stopped by the cloak room where the women gathered their coats.

While Emily's mother went to ask the porter to order them a taxi, Emily pressed a small piece of paper into Walter's hand.

Outside, the drizzle had become a cold rain. They stood under the entrance, wondering when the pickup limousine would arrive.

"Young man", the mother said, smiling at him in a way that he felt sure was meant to be encouraging, "you brought us luck. Very soon, you will have your prize." She glanced at her daughter, and Emily gave Walter an honest smile.

"We should see each other again, Emily," Walter suggested.

"Why don't you bet on it?" she replied coquettishly. Then, she said, "Call me tomorrow. I would like to see you again."

Von Rundstedt's Plan

It was raining heavily, and a cold storm was blowing from Brittany toward the east. Slowly, the Horch limousine turned into the rondel and stopped at the barrier just before the gate of the post.

Lang, with Field Marshal Rommel in the back, tapped his forehead with two fingers, which the guard acknowledged with a friendly nod and permission to enter. The barrier opened, and the car turned onto a cobblestone street leading to the parking lot of the Prince Villa. This was the home of Commander-in-Chief of Army Group West, Field Marshal von Rundstedt. The elderly and most respected Field Marshal of the Reich had asked Rommel to lunch.

Rommel was not in the best of spirits, though. The wintry weather had turned the streets of Northern France into muddy slopes with meter-deep potholes. He also saw it as a sign of the other officers' hubris that his building of the Atlantic Wall had never been acknowledged by anyone in the General Staff. Besides, he still had not received proper help, as promised by the Fuehrer. And now he had to come here to the old Field Marshal? It was referred to as lunch. *Very well*, Rommel thought, *I'll see if I can reach a consensus with the old man.*

The door was opened for Rommel, and two young men in black gloves and steel helmets escorted the Field Marshal through the library hall and directly into the dining room. Rommel nodded. Everything looked quite posh. On the turquoise dining table were lighted silver candelabra next to the open red and white wine bottles. The tall Louis-Seis chairs were being placed by young maidservants in black maid dresses and knotted hair next to the tables. At the end of the room, Rommel saw food covered by a huge silver lid being pushed on a trolley.

In oversized, wingback chairs sat two men in front of a fireplace. They turned to Rommel and smiled at him in a friendly manner. One of the men was his host, Field Marshal Erich von Rundstedt. The old Field Marshal rose, walked slowly up to Rommel, and nodded to him. "Welcome to Headquarters OB West."

Rommel tapped his heels together, raised his arm, and nodded as well. "Heil Hitler."

"Don't be so formal, Herr Rommel. Here, it's only about the food," von Rundstedt said ironically and showed the way to the chairs. "Before I beckon you to the table, allow me to introduce an old friend and an excellent soldier, Herr Emil Leeb, head of the Army Weapons Department."

The two men shook hands.

"And thereby may all formalities be dispensed with," von Rundstedt said. "Let us sit down."

As if with the push of a button, the staff ladies appeared and poured a glass of wine for each of them. Silently, the gentlemen toasted each other, moving the corner of their mouths in the old German way, as if the wine was unbearable.

"Now please do tell, Herr Rommel," von Rundstedt opened the conversation. "Africa was some time ago. Have you settled in well, here in France?"

Rommel glanced to the side, folding his hands. "Well, as you surely know, I am fully absorbed in my work. That's what I live for, after all. It's very important."

"Yes, and as the Fuehrer's favorite general, it was only a matter of time before you were given a full-fledged task. Isn't that so?"

Rommel dabbed his mouth with the folded napkin. "With all due respect to your sense of irony, it's not about my person. The construction and effectiveness of the Atlantic Wall will determine Germany's fate."

The old Field Marshal stuffed a huge piece of meat into his mouth. He stared straight into Rommel's eyes, and his constant chewing made it hard to see if he was smiling or simply chewing hard. Finally, he paused and grinned.

"So, the Atlantic Wall. Will you actually finish it?"

"You can rely on me and all the resources I have!"

Herr Leeb leaned forward. "Herr Rommel, may I ask you something? What resources do you have at your disposal?"

"As you know, Army Group B reports to me. There are many things at my disposal."

"True. But if the enemy lands, which weapons do you primarily intend to use?"

"I have a plan. Small arms will play a major role. Tell me, what do you think of American MG-50? It's an excellent heavy machine gun, unique in its combination of range, penetration, usability, and speed of fire."

Leeb laughed out loud. "My dear Rommel, I know the MG-50. Our enemies were so friendly at Dieppe and in Italy that they showed it to me. But the MG is way too heavy for infantry troops to carry by hand and bring it forward."

"Maybe Herr Rommel intends to mount this on mobile trucks or something similar," interjected von Rundstedt.

"I mean," Rommel continued in a slightly abrupt tone, "that the MG-50 would be a perfect weapon if it could be set up in small pillow-box bunkers to strike enemy landing craft when they are unloading. It would also be suitable for fighting light vehicles, such as American trucks or jeeps. It's an excellent infantry weapon. I wish we had something like it."

Leeb waved his hand dismissively. "We don't have anything like that, nor is it possible."

"Not possible?" Rommel's face blushed. "Excuse me, but I think I'm talking to exactly the right person. And since we're sitting here together, I'd like to officially ask you to investigate the design of the American MG, and if possible, reproduce it quickly and send it to me in quantities."

Von Rundstedt shook his head. "Herr Rommel, what you're talking about is nonsense. You should know that it takes many months to obtain approval for new weapons. Besides, there is the issue of ammunition. Since when have you become so naive? Have another glass of wine."

Field Marshal Rommel pressed his lips together as his rage started to mount.

"Herr von Rundstedt is right," said Leeb. "The MG 50 is a good weapon, but impractical to introduce into the Wehrmacht. And in such a short time? It's not that easy. But I shall attend to it, Herr Rommel."

"Look, Herr Rommel," von Rundstedt began as he poured himself more wine and brightened up, "we are open to discussion here. I'm the Commander-in-Chief West, and I make the decisions. Now, help yourself."

"Herr von Rundstedt, I don't want to sound like a know-it-all, but I think that with the right selection of weapons, which we *can* realistically secure, we have a very good chance."

"All right. We'll see what we can do about the panzers."

"Then, every hundred meters we build a pillow-box, equipped with MG 42s, plus hundreds of 2-cm Flakvierling Model 38s. Also, an artillery gun at least every hundred yards" Rommel said.

"No, no," Von Rundstedt dabbed his mouth again. "You will never get that approved, not in that quantity."

"A whole Flak corps is standing futilely near Paris. They need to be sent where they will be needed," Rommel countered.

"Why should the Reichsmarschall and Supreme Commander of the Luftwaffe, Goering, listen to you?"

"The Eighty-eight is well-known, and we had great success in Africa with it. Goering will remember that. We could contact Goering together. Then, he has to react."

"Didn't you know, Rommel?" continued von Rundstedt in a smug tone. "Most of the Eighty-eight are being sent to the Reich... for the protection of facilities. Six dozen units have been shipped to Berlin alone since the beginning of the year."

Rommel became increasingly agitated: "That doesn't matter. I urge you to work with me. It's not just about the Eighty-eights or the MGs; we should all agree on a common strategy."

"A good approach, the first sensible thing I've heard from you," added Leeb with a grin.

Rommel took a deep breath. "Herr Field Marshal, you're the most senior Field Marshal of the Wehrmacht. You command 60 divisions here in the West. The main responsibility here lies with you. I have to ask you to work with me. Help me secure the Flaks and give me the panzers."

Von Rundstedt's gaze darkened. "My dear Herr Rommel, allow me to tell you a bit about the actual situation of my supposed 60 divisions, about the mighty force here in the West that I supposedly command. See, only a few of these divisions could be considered first-class. No more than 15 of them have either the equipment or the personnel to warrant their being classed as a division. Aside from the panzer and parachute divisions that are still being sent the fittest troops and most modern weapons, the bulk of the infantry divisions are miserable skeletons of fighting units. As you know, they are sitting deep in their bunkers on the coast. They are equipped with a hodgepodge of foreign artillery and they rely on horses and bicycles for their mobility. They're formed chiefly of personnel from older age groups and convalescents from the Russian front."

"But as Supreme Commander West, do you not have influence over Hitler?"

"Only on paper am I the Supreme Commander in the West. In reality, I have no decisive influence with the Luftwaffe and the Navy in the preparation of the defense. And Hitler or the Wehrmacht High Command interfere in both major and minor issues. You might not believe it, Rommel, but in reality, I have only enough power to change the guards here at my headquarters."

"Yes, and we've known that for a while." Rommel looked inexplicably slightly amused. That's why we should work together, according to my alternative plan, which clearly stands out from that of the Fuehrer. I know what I'm doing, Field Marshal."

"The problem is," Leeb added, "that to strike back a landing right at the water's edge, you need to have all the forces, as well as the best weapons and troops, and probably panzers, in large numbers up at the front.

"Exactly!"

"Yes, but you would need to know exactly where the enemy is landing. Only then would you be able to amass all the forces in the right place."

"That's what I intend to do."

"But do you know where the enemy will land?"

"Of course not, but there is a growing presumption that it will be at the Somme or Normandy."

Field Marshal von Rundstedt shrugged. "A presumption. You don't know any more than everyone else."

"I believe the Navy and Luftwaffe, and they still have the best information. I talked with Luftflotte 3 and Dönitz. They say Normandy."

"Okay, but they don't have a crystal ball either, so we need reserves for a counterstrike."

"When they land, it will be too late. You don't need reserves. Instead, give me everything you have. Place the mobile troops under my command. We don't need to do it officially. Just move the troops over to me. Believe me, I will get it done."

"Herr Rommel? Hello, Herr Rommel?" Von Rundstedt leaned over the table towards Rommel. "May I remind you of Fuehrer's instruction Number 51. You may also have heard of it, and as far as I can remember, it says that "by summer at the latest," we can expect an attack on the western front of Europe. In order to be prepared for this "decisive landing battle," the fighting force in the West must be increased to the detriment of other fronts. Movable reserves are to be made available in France. This is an order from the Fuehrer! This also means that if the enemy still manages to land by amassing their forces, we need to hit them with a counterattack led with the greatest possible force. And that's only possible with panzers from my reserve, Herr Rommel, a very flexible reserve of panzers set up in the hinterland. Do I need to say that any clearer?"

"It's very clear, Herr Field Marshal. Still, we have to stop the enemy from landing. My experiences in North Africa and from what I know from Italy prove that the enemy air force will appear with such great numbers and armament that they'll make any movement of panzers and reserves impossible. They have fighter-bombers that will shoot every panzer from above. They'll attack us like a swarm of locusts."

Von Rundstedt shook his head in resignation. "Herr Rommel, there must be a way. As you know, I will try everything, and my plan is to support you. But, like everyone else, we have a duty to obey the Fuehrer's instructions, and a panzer army must stand in reserve! However, I agree with you that the right weapons must be on the front line of the coastal defenses. Do you agree, Leeb?"

"Of course. It's just that I can't help with 50- caliber machine gun."

"What about the enemy's heavy ship artillery?" von Rundstedt questioned, changing topics.

"There will be losses on our side, without question," Rommel conceded. "But if the pillow-box bunkers are not hit directly, then our defenses will stand."

Von Rundstedt sat down again and smiled. "And how should I convince the powerful gentleman in the light blue Luftwaffe uniform to go along with this? He only listens to the Fuehrer."

"Yes, the Reichsmarschall, Goering, is a gangster in his own right," added Rommel angrily. "I cannot rely on his Luftwaffe, and I don't have any hopes about that."

"Be careful with what you say, Herr Rommel."

"I know. But I'm talking openly here. You're the senior member amongst the Field Marshals. You can try."

"I'll talk with him. But I can't get the panzers out of my head. You want to use the panzer army right at the front?"

"Yes, as close to the beach as possible."

"They won't stay hidden from the enemy. The German armored troops need to be held in rear positions and attack only after the Allies have gained a foothold. Maybe we could put some panzers here and there at the front of the beach, but in very small numbers. Maybe I'll go along with that."

"We need panzers at the front if the enemy manages to break through somewhere. And as I said, considering the clear Allied air superiority, any warfare from the rear is hopeless. The panzer formations must be stationed as close as possible to the presumed landing areas."

The old Field Marshal lowered his head. "One question, Herr Rommel: what do you think will happen if we actually beat them back?"

"Then, we negotiate for peace. We owe it to our people and, strictly speaking, to humanity. Speaking frankly, I am anything but an adherent of the Nazis."

The old Field Marshal swallowed. "Be careful, Herr Rommel. And all the best."

In parting, the two Field Marshals silently shook hands.

Lang had rarely seen the Field Marshal so silent. On the way home, the Field Marshal had only one recurring thought. Could he really rely on the support of the old Field Marshal von Rundstedt?

The Casino

Elmer was sitting on a bench across the street from the casino, drinking a bottle of beer when his friend Walter arrived. A steady drizzle was falling as Walter sat down, pulled out his cigarettes, and offered Elmer one. The other man took one, and they sat with the unlit cigarettes dangling from their lips. "We should head to that bar on the other side of the barracks," Elmer said after a long stretch of silence.

"I thought we were going to the casino tonight," Walter said, unable to hide his annoyance. "We've been planning this for weeks."

"I just want to go find a girl," Elmer said. "You know how many of them broads are interested in us GIs. That bar down by the barracks leaves me enough time to spend in the company of a lady before I have to get back."

"Those girls aren't ladies," Walter said with a derisive snort. "And you're a fool if you think that they are."

The fact that Elmer didn't look hurt in the least made Walter mad. His naïve friend nodded amiably. "They're still nice to look at," he said.

"They're from the gutter," Walter said, venom dripping from his voice. "This war, us being here in England… Unless you find something that's worth doing here, it's all a huge waste of time. I don't even know if this war is worth it for America."

"Why is this war a waste of time?" Elmer asked, irritated. "It's going to be a sweet ride all the way to France."

"Sure, but why not trying to make something out of it? I mean, there's got to be something in this for us, right?"

"You are a strange fellow, you know that?" Elmer observed as he stood.

"Why do you say that?"

Ignoring the question, Elmer said, "Last time, you told me you had a brother over there in France, serving in the Wehrmacht."

"So?"

"Are you going to look for him?"

"Should I try to find him after the landing? He must have become a Nazi. God help me if I see him again before the war ends. I would question him, for sure. "

"All right. But If he were standing in front of you, with a gun pointed at you to block you from invading Nazi territory, would you shoot him?"

For a second, Walter looked sideways. "I guess so. Every active fighter is a Nazi. Brother or not, I would shoot. Yeah, you could say so."

Walter thought about his brother a few seconds longer, and the thoughts disturbed him. *Why did Elmer have to bring that up?*

Elmer took another sip from the bottle. "Could be that your brother is stationed in the back. Besides, not everybody fights. He could be a cook, you know?

"Yeah, I know, and we'll see what happens. But let's stop this nonsense talk and go over to the casino, right?"

Elmer shook his head. "I'm going to the bar. Are you coming with me or not?"

"Not," Walter replied. "I'm going to the casino like we planned."

"Suit yourself," Elmer said as he stuffed his hands into his pockets and headed off down the street.

Walter lit his cigarette and stewed over his friend's departure. He couldn't believe the nerve Elmer had. Walter had at least tried to look like a gentleman today. With his best jacket and pressed shirt, he planned to make his case, to find someone suitable and lucrative, right there in the casino.

After watching the large, middle-aged woman in an oversized black dress and Edwardian hat lose several rounds in a row, Walter approached her and said, "Would you mind if I offered you a few pointers, ma'am?"

The woman gave him a doubtful look, but nodded. Walter leaned close to her and started to whisper tricks he had learned from his own days as a fairly successful gambler. When the woman won the next round, she declared, "You must be my good luck charm. Sit here beside my daughter, Emily. I'll let you know if I need any more pointers."

Walter, delighted that his plan had worked so well, sat down next to the younger woman, Emily and gave her his most charming smile. She smiled back shyly, and he was pleased to see that she was as beautiful up close as she had seemed from across the room.

Her blue eyes shone and her blond bob curled softly around her ears and chin.

"Are you American?" the girl asked.

"I am," he said. "I'm Walter. Walter Schmidt."

"I'm Emily," the girl said.

"What are you doing here tonight, Emily?" he asked.

She rolled her eyes demurely and tipped her chin toward her mother. "She was invited to come by a very minor gentleman who runs things in this town. She thinks it will improve our social standing to be seen with him."

"And where is he now?" Walter asked. He could see that Emily's mother had good sense when it came to social class.

"Probably getting sloshed at the bar," she said.

"Hmmm," Walter commented with a frown. That didn't do him any good. He liked what he saw in this girl. She was hot and direct. He thought that being seeing with her and her mother made good sense. The two of them chatted until the older woman was done playing.

"Are you in a gambling mood?" Emily's mother asked Walter.

"Always am," he replied, bowing slightly.

She smirked and nodded. "Let's go over to the roulette table. I could need a lucky and noticing win tonight."

"Mom! "Emily jumped forward. "You gambled it all away, didn't you?"

Walter didn't want to listen, but it was still quite amusing hearing them arguing. He followed them and they were hardly seated before the mother beckoned him to make a bet and spin.

The dealer lady chuckled and shoved a stack of colored chips toward Walter. The result was a shock. Nobody, not even Walter could believe that he had won. Everybody burst out in excitement.

Emily's mother seemed proud, but then, she noticed the time.

"Oh, dear, Emily," she said, pressing her hand to her chest. "We need to hurry home before your father returns."

"I'll walk you out," Walter offered.

Emily took his right arm, and her mother took his left. The three of them stopped by the cloak room where the women gathered their coats.

While Emily's mother went to ask the porter to order them a taxi, Emily pressed a small piece of paper into Walter's hand.

Outside, the drizzle had become a cold rain. They stood under the entrance, wondering when the pickup limousine would arrive.

"Young man", the mother said, smiling at him in a way that he felt sure was meant to be encouraging, "you brought us luck. Very soon, you will have your prize." She glanced at her daughter, and Emily gave Walter an honest smile.

"We should see each other again, Emily," Walter suggested.

"Why don't you bet on it?" she replied coquettishly. Then, she said, "Call me tomorrow. I would like to see you again."

Active Leisure

Helmut knelt beside the old staff officer who still was lying in the sand in half-sleep or perhaps in a half-sober state.

"Sir, something is not right. "Helmut patted the man on the shoulder. "I saw flashing lights all over the horizon. And do you hear the sounds? Airplanes, but they're not bombers. "

The old staff officer turned around and shook his head. "Nah, no bombers nor the Luftwaffe. Maybe enemy transport planes. Who knows?"

Helmut nodded. "Maybe gliders, or even enemy commandos."

"When they come, they'll end up behind our positions. Paratroopers, if I'd had to guess."

"That would mean it's going to start today. But the weather is too bad for that, I think."

The old soldier shrugged. "Exactly. There might be lights and planes, but with this swell, the weather is almost stormy. I don't think it'll happen today. So, take it easy. Let's sleep a little more. It's too early."

"Sergeant, can I have some of your reserve… you know?"

The veteran's face darkened. "My good cognac? That was my share. I only have half a bottle left. And if they actually come today, I'll need the rest, okay? "

"It's a cool night, and I'll get fresh juice from the locals tomorrow, okay?"

The old soldier nodded and turned around for another round of sleep.

Helmut took the bottle and emptied the hip flask all at once. Immediately, the pleasant heat shot into body and head. He sat with his back against the cold bunker wall. He felt confused. Why did he have to think about Nicole right now? The woman was a curse. No, she was not so bad of a person. But the whole situation with her traitor-friends and family… He took a photo out of his pocket. She was still as pretty as in his daily memory. No question, the young thing had somewhat traumatized him. A few weeks ago, they were still a secret couple, meeting secretly in the soldier's club. Helmut closed his eyes and saw her face again.

She stood nervously by the front door, her dress modest but becoming. Nicole's face lit up when she saw him approach, and although they were both skittish to begin, once the food had arrived and the drinks were flowing, so was the conversation.

"Your German is excellent," Helmut said. "I'm sorry my French is so poor."

"Well, I was working as a teacher before I came here," Nicole said, sipping from her wine glass. "Language is my forte."

"So, you said that you came here with your family?" Helmut asked.

Nicole sighed. "Yes. I moved to Normandy recently along with my immediate family because some of my extended family members in northern France have been deported to Germany. We didn't see them often, in the past, and now… I don't know if I'll ever see them again. My uncle has a dairy farm, you see? Papa said we needed to come straight away, to help out, because that's what my uncle would have done for him if he were in trouble."

"It's good to have family you can rely on." Helmut nodded, wondering who she meant by 'we'. Did she have brothers or sisters? Nicole seemed nice enough, but French boys… they could be puffed up, impassioned by what was going on. If Nicole did have a brother, it could spell trouble.

"So, tell me about you," Nicole said, picking up her wine glass. "Let's not talk about depressing things. Tell me about your life before the war."

"Well, I'm not just a soldier and gunner for the Flak company, if that's what you're thinking. There's more to me than that. Before the war I wanted to enroll at university. I was eager to study and wanted to get a degree in engineering." He took a mouthful of food, casting his mind back to that time that seemed so long ago. At the same time, Helmut was considering if he should be talking this way, giving away so many details about himself. After all, Nicole was his secret girlfriend—the less she knew about his real life, the better. He thought of a meaningless, throwaway comment to distract her. "My main hobby is my motorcycle, the one I rode every day before the war. It's still there, at home. At least, I hope it is! I have a French Motobécane motorcycle."

"Oh really? My brother has the same type!" Nicole said in astonishment. "He has an interest in engineering, too, actually. I think you guys would get on well."

"Yeah, sounds like it." Helmut nodded, wondering if that were true. Brothers could be overly protective of their sisters, particularly if their sister's boyfriends just so happened to be dating 'the enemy'. He didn't think a meeting would be so wise.

"I'd love to introduce you to my brother," she said smiling. "Seriously. We can pretend that there is nothing strange at all about a nice French girl asking a German officer over to her house to meet her family. It will be like… well, like days that I can't even remember now. Before the war, before all this…"

She gestured around at the room filled with men in uniforms.

"Well, why not?" Helmut smiled, his wild streak speaking to him louder and more clearly than the little voice in his head that was telling him to *be careful, be cautious*. After all, on paper it looked like a terrible idea, but maybe there was a particular reason he should agree. Maybe there was something he could find out, a secret he could uncover that would help the war effort.

Helmut and Nicole had a lovely evening, and their secrecy remained intact—neither Herbert nor Thomas had the faintest idea where Helmut had been that night. He couldn't get her off his mind, even though he knew it was a folly, and it wouldn't work out. It was a few nights later when he received a note from Nicole, inviting him to come and meet her… and her family.

Rising Storm

The connection was bad, but Rommel undoubtedly recognized the Fuehrer's voice. "Yes, my Fuehrer. I am very pleased that the heavy MG's and more light Flaks will support my efforts."

"Have you positioned the forces correctly?"

"My Fuehrer, we have managed to build a small-caliber 2-cm Flak every two hundred meters in the region of Normandy and south of the Somme and to construct a tower with an Eighty-eight roughly every five hundred meters."

"I already know that, Rommel. What else do you need?"

"Well, forgive me, my Fuehrer, but I desperately need the Panzer Army."

"Herr Rommel, the Panzer Army remains in reserve and under the command of Field Marshal Von Rundstedt. You have to live with what you have."

"My Fuehrer, without the panzers I cannot guarantee anything!"

"I'll tell you what, Rommel. When the enemy actually lands and proceeds to break through your defense line, and if Rundstedt can spare a few panzer divisions without compromising the reserve, and if we become more confident of where they'll attack, then you can personally request two, maybe three, divisions from me. And regarding the landing zone, once you have more information, please get through to me."

"Yes, my Fuehrer."

Rommel held the receiver for a few seconds after the Fuehrer had hung up. He felt the anger rising in him.

"Speidel, I can only get three additional panzer divisions at the most. And I can only request them in case of an attack"

"Unbelievable, I have not seen a bigger dilettante than him."

Rommel nodded thoughtfully. "Well, we already know that."

"But we've still made some progress, especially with the small towers and the Eighty-eight mounted on top of them."

"As much as we could, Speidel. They're difficult to disguise, easy to disable, and many of the operators will end up sacrificing themselves, but for the first few hours of landing waves they'll do their job. But the matter regarding the panzers is still not certain. Hitler only sent me three divisions and said I can request the rest!"

Speidel just shrugged his shoulders. "Better than nothing."

"I've had enough, Speidel. What do you think, do I need to file a written application in the Reich Chancellery when the enemy lands?"

"What else can you do?"

"I have to go to Hitler and explain the situation to him. I have to talk to him alone. He only hears things from the criminals around him."

"Do you really believe that?"

"I know that you and your friends see things differently, Speidel, but I don't want to stand here as the commander who led his soldiers to the slaughterhouse."

"But at least you got the small arms you wanted. Maybe that's enough."

"Maybe, but maybe not."

"There are other options. Take the plunge politically, if you understand what I'm saying."

"I know exactly what you're talking about. And you're right, but not now. Anyone who acts now risks letting everything collapse. But if we succeed in repelling the enemy, then I'll act, Speidel! But another thing: as you know, I have been on the road for almost a year without interruption, conducting almost daily inspections far away from my command. Don't be surprised if I ask for a few days holiday from Rundstedt."

"You should do that, Herr Field Marshal. With this weather, we don't expect a major attack for another few days."

"I'll try. And maybe the Fuehrer will change his mind about the panzers at the last minute. We'll see. "

"The Fuehrer has to change his mind one way or the other, Herr Field Marshal."

Rommel shook his head. "Be very careful, Speidel. No more political comments. Believe me; it's better that way."

The Family Proposal

The next day, when Walter called, a man answered the phone and gruffly told him that Emily was unavailable to come to the phone. The same happened the next day. And the next. Then the next few days were filled with training drills, which made Walter think that the actual combat would start sooner rather than later, though he still had no proof.

By the time he finally managed to get a message to her, it had been nearly a week since they had last seen each other. They agreed to meet in a park near her home where she often went to walk. There was a small fountain that continued to run even in the depth of winter. That was where they were to meet.

It had begun to rain when Emily arrived, but she insisted that they walk anyway. They made their way to a small gazebo where they could take shelter from the icy spray coming from the sky. They talked of trivial things, neither one ever mentioning the war. When it was time to bid her goodbye, Walter felt a pang of regret. He was almost certain now that he would be sent into combat soon enough.

This pattern continued over the next week, but then, one day, she said something that stopped him in his tracks. "Perhaps we could go to your place next week," she said.

Walter hemmed and hawed as he tried to think of a way out of it. He had wanted to kiss her before she had suggested that. He knew that her father did not want her being courted by an American, and a few casual dates would enrage the man. Walter wasn't even sure if he wanted to get that deeply involved with her, either, but Emily kept finding ways to draw him in.

Now, Walter had a new worry to add to his list. That list seemed to grow longer with each passing day. He had to find a place that could be his for a few hours, somewhere he could bring a girl like Emily.

He asked some of his fellow soldiers, and it turned out that one captain had rented a set of rooms down the street from the barracks. Through some wheeling and dealing, Walter managed to find the guy in the canteen.

"How much would you charge for me to rent your rooms for a couple of hours next Thursday?" Walter asked.

The man smirked at him, wiped his mouth on his sleeve, and said, "Fifty bucks."

Walter frowned, but nodded. "Deal."

By the time he brought Emily there the next Thursday, Walter was wound into a ball of worry. "It's charming," she pronounced as she seated herself on a chair.

"Uh, thanks," Walter said as he sat down beside her. They made small talk, but all the while, Walter was wondering why she had wanted him to bring her here. He was too confused to ask, though, with his mind flying to the possible perils of combat every other second. The town had become busy, with trucks and tanks being loaded into ships. There was something coming up bigtime. He just couldn't get rid of that nasty though. *This stupid war.*

Just as he had managed to get the thoughts under control and was leaning over to kiss her, there was a pounding on the door. Walter thought that perhaps his contact had forgotten to tell someone that the apartment was in use that afternoon. Who knew what the other man did in his spare time?

"Excuse me just a moment," he said to Emily.

The minute he opened the door, though, a tall, older man brushed past him. "Emily," he said in a voice that dripped with carefully controlled anger.

"Father!" Emily exclaimed.

"I told you that you were forbidden to see this Yankee soldier," he said. "We are going home, now!" With that, he took hold of his daughter's upper arm and marched her out of the rooms. Walter just watched them go, wondering if he should say something, and if so, what? He was relieved that Emily's father hadn't punched him in the face or, worse, reported him to one of his superiors, though how the man had known he was in the army and here in this place, he didn't know. He and Emily hadn't talked about it at all, so Walter had no idea what she knew.

Ridiculous bunch. Maybe one day I'll return and shoot this Brit for nothing, he thought. Walter returned to the barracks and refused to speak to anyone for the rest of the day. Even though he hadn't been sure how he felt about Emily, now that he was sure that he would never see her again, he felt his heart squeezing in his chest.

He was shocked the next day when he received a note summoning him to Emily's house. Though he was unsure what to expect, he was somehow thrilled to be invited to the family's home, which he knew from Emily was in the nicest part of town. He hoped the old man wouldn't make a mistake. Because if he does, it'll cost him. Embarkment could be today or tomorrow, so he wouldn't take shit from anybody.

When Emily opened the door, she was clearly surprised to see him in his uniform. He had been careful to wear classier clothes when they were together.

"Come in, Walter," she said, taking his arm. "My father wants to talk to you."

Those words put fear in his heart, but he allowed her to lead him into her father's study. "Ah, yes, Walter Schmidt," Emily's father said. "Come in. Come in. Emily, leave us for now."

Emily gave Walter's arm a squeeze of support, and then, reluctantly left the room. When the door had closed behind her, her father gestured for Walter to sit down.

"I'm Charles Templeton," he said. "I am not pleased that you were seeing my daughter behind my back."

"I…" Walter began to say.

Charles held up a hand. "However, my daughter tells me that you have ambitions beyond this war. She says that you want to become a hotel operator, or you want even to become an architect?"

Walter cleared his throat. "That is true," he said.

"To tell you the truth, I've always admired the early work of Speer." Charles paused, but before Walter could respond with his surprise, the older man went on, "I have a client at the bank who runs an architecture firm in London. After the war, I would be more than happy to recommend you to him as a junior partner."

Walter couldn't believe what he was hearing. He was speechless, managing only to splutter out a thank you. The tall Brit silenced him again. "There is one condition," he said.

"Anything," Walter said, still amazed at what the man was offering.

"When you get back from the war, you must marry my daughter, and I mean it."

Walter barely suppressed his laughter. *Who is this guy kidding?* he thought. But he said nothing and the condition hung in the air between them. Walter knew that there was no way to get what he wanted unless he accepted, but was it worth marrying the girl?

"Do we have an agreement?" the father asked as he held out a hand for Walter to shake.

Walter ran his hand through his hair and then, extended it to the man. "We do, sir."

Emily was overjoyed as Walter headed back to the barracks. He couldn't believe what he had just agreed to. But when he got back, he immediately knew that something was wrong. His fellow soldiers were rushing around, getting ready for… something.

"The embarkment is happening now!" Elmer called, shoving a knapsack at Walter.

As Walter got ready to go, his mind whirled with unfinished thoughts. This was it. It wasn't in his hands anymore. Would he survive? He was fairly certain there was no way he would survive once he got into combat, and that would make the agreement he'd made with Charles Templeton all for naught.

He tried to think of all the ways he could get out of going, but he was shuttled along with the rest of the men. As he headed down toward the docks, he heard someone calling his name. He turned to see Emily pushing her way through the crush of other women coming to see the men off.

"You come back to me, Walter Schmidt!" she yelled. "If you don't, I'll kill myself."

Walter turned around and stared at her in disbelief. *We're not that close yet*, he thought.

Emily stood close to Walter, her eyes betraying honest desperation. "I don't want anything to happen to you; that's all."

For a fraction of a second, a dark shadow flitted across Walter's gaze, something squeezing into his stomach like an unknown force. He took a deep breath. "Don't worry about me," he croaked out.

Emily held him by both forearms, only looking at his nervous eyes. *Where is the self-confident man? This isn't the man who I know,* she thought.

"It will go all right. My regiment has to leave tonight. Don't ask me where to."

Emily just nodded thoughtfully.

"Come back well. That's all I'm asking of you."

Before Walter could say anything more, he was moved along to the boat, and that same evening, the fleet set sail toward Normandy with Walter not knowing what his future looked like, or if he even had one. The embarkment had started, and Walter had to go with his unit. He knew he had no choice even though he would have sold his soul to the devil to stay in England, taking Emily's father up on his offer.

A hazy mist hung low over the water as the ship departed from the dock. As a fresh wave of terror took hold of Walter, he realized that the weather served as an apt metaphor for his unknown future. All he could do was hold the promise of Emily and her family waiting for him when he came back from France. Pressing that thought to the front of his mind, Walter felt the corner of his mouth lift into a half smile.

Headquarters Army Group B - May 1944

"Speidel, a small miracle has happened," Rommel said. "In spite of all the contradictions in the overall strategy, von Rundstedt and I have come together and found common solutions. You know, the old Field Marshal still has excellent personal contacts, and together, we've managed to actually transfer several hundred extra Flak regiments from the Reich to the Western Front and station them on the coast."

"It was high time, Herr Field Marshal. The signs are increasing daily that the Anglo Americans will land soon."

"It's the end of May, but I'm relatively satisfied. The pillow-boxes are nearly all finished and, as planned, all the old MG 34 infantry divisions are now equipped with the stronger and more effective MG-42. The big bunkers, which were originally planned and started by Hitler with heavy anti-ship guns are, as we foresaw, still mostly unfinished. And I'll tell you honestly, Speidel, I did not bother with them."

"I understand, but still we have made some progress, especially with the small concrete towers that lie in a chain and the Eighty-eight mounted on top of them."

"As much as we could, Speidel. They're difficult to disguise, easy to disable, and many of the operators will end up sacrificing themselves, but for the first few hours of landing waves they'll do their job. But the matter regarding the panzers is still not certain. Hitler only sent me three divisions and said I can request the rest!"

"Unbelievable, I have not seen a bigger dilettante than him."

Rommel nodded thoughtfully. "Well, we already know that. But another thing, Speidel: as you know, I have been on the road for almost a year without interruption, almost daily inspections, far away from my command. Don't be surprised if I ask for a few days holiday from Rundstedt."

"You should do that, Herr Field Marshal. With this weather, we don't expect a major attack for another few days."

"I'll try. And maybe the Fuehrer will change his mind about the panzers at the last minute. We'll see. "

"The Fuehrer has to change his mind one way or the other, Herr Field Marshal."

Rommel shook his head. "Be very careful, Speidel. No more political comments. Believe me, it's better that way."

D-DAY

Helmut pressed the binoculars close to his eyes. The nascent gray morning light only revealed veils of cloud on the horizon. The horizon was nothing more than a nondescript wall. Slowly, he waved the binoculars from left to right. Suddenly, out of nowhere, a broad string of lights flashed on the horizon. There appeared to be more: ten, no, twenty, at least. Then, he saw the lightning. "I'll be damned," he stuttered. The flashes were numerous, appearing like a single line of fire.

"Enemy naval artillery ahead. The enemy is opening fire!" he shouted. "To your post!" Then, he heard the well-known, increasingly louder whistling. "Attention impact!" As soon as the words were out of his mouth, all hell broke loose.

Impacts. Helmut thought his eardrums had burst, and yet, in that second, he felt something strange, more than a thought. *You won't survive this.* He started praying. *God let me get through this, and I'll do whatever You want.* The explosions came closer.

But the armed attack from the ship's artillery came so suddenly and so fast, that between one second and the other, it was over.

Smoke. Silence. The men scrambled to their feet. Everyone who had binoculars stared at the horizon. There was more movement now—lights and small moving shadows, thousands of them.

"Hold your fire!" yelled the sergeant, pacing nervously back and forth behind the men. Moving to the left of Helmut's Flak position in the pillow-box, the men made their way to the MG-42, moving the barrels right through the hatch, clearly marking their runs toward the sea. Soon, they would launch their test fire. The little fat sergeant puffed up into the bunker. "Hey, you in there, no test fire. Let them get close." Again, he trudged back to the Flak. *This madman's making everyone unnecessarily nervous*, Helmut thought. *We know what let them get close means.*

"The artillery fire can come back any second," mumbled the sergeant from behind.

In the distance, the dots grew larger. The craft looked like dashes swirling up and down. Helmut was sitting in his Flakvierling. He turned the positional wheel until he had the first ships in his sights. He nodded to his two loaders. "How many replacement magazines, Herbert?"

"Forty-one, plus the loaded one."

"Thomas?"

"Not counted, but around 50."

"You others?"

"Forty, 60 ... the same ...," the men answered.

"Give Herbert some. You already know that one magazine lasts for six seconds. Reload immediately."

"All right. Incendiary rounds?"

"Only those! We don't need the armor-piercing projectiles yet. We'll shoot at the panzers later." Helmut knew he could rely on his team, but now, everything had to run like clockwork. There was no room for error. His eyes were fixed. And there they came. "Get ready! The landing craft are already coming up at the front."

Suddenly, the heavily breathing sergeant was beside the Flak. "You at the Flak are the first to open fire. Will you let the ships within six hundred meters?"

"That's what it looks like to us, sergeant," Helmut replied calmly, picking up his binoculars. "Landing craft, with destroyers behind them. At most 1,000 meters."

"Hold," the sergeant grunted again.

Helmut aimed the Flak barrels almost horizontally. One degree lower, and the cannons would hit the landing craft exactly on the waterline. *Shred them and sink them* was the phrase that rushed into Helmut's mind.

Somewhere to the left of his position, Helmut heard nervous MG test fire, then silence again.

The armada of landing craft sloshed even closer. The horizon was black with ships. Helmut thought he recognized much larger landing craft on the right. *Those are the big boys loaded with panzers and trucks. If they get to us, we'll barely have any projectiles for panzers.* With a raised hand, he briefly gestured to his men. "It's about to start. Ready?"

Thomas nodded. Herbert was already holding the next magazine with both hands ready to load it.

Very lightly, Helmut's right hand pressed on the trigger. In the iron crosshairs, two landing craft in close proximity to each other rushed straight to the beach. Any second, the first explosion could come. *Eight hundred meters*, Helmut told himself. The landing craft were now clearly visible. Even the camouflage was recognizable. The crosshairs were now aimed at the ship's ramp, just above the waterline. The first Rommelspargel, the metal rails in the sea furnished with explosive mines, would stop the first boats that came within 500 meters. There the ships should get entangled and build a line of fire. That's how it was planned.

The men held their fire for a few more seconds. *Let them come,* the voice in Helmut's head ordered. *Seven hundred meters.*

Still, silence. Helmut's eyes were fixed on the two landing craft through the crosshairs. They rocked strongly, the swell of the sea obviously stronger than was recognizable from land. *The left boat first,* Helmut thought. His foot tapped the pedal, and the cannon aimed directly at the ramp of the left boat. Helmut whispered, "Hold, another 10 seconds. Nine, eight …" A few hundred yards to the left and right, he heard deep rattling; the other 2-cm Flak had already opened fire. *A few seconds more ...*

Slowly and steadily, Helmut pushed the trigger, right up to the breaking point.

"Hold your fire. That goes for the Flak!" The fat sergeant stood behind him again. Suddenly, a whistle came from somewhere. *The fat little idiot is destroying more here than the enemy out there,* Helmut thought falteringly.

Violent explosions sounded behind their position as bomb blasts spat smoke into the sky. Then came heavy ship artillery and more thundering explosions. Helmut quickly raised his binoculars. Not more than 600 meters, the armada was landing. "We will not let our cannon be shot away from under our arse!" shouted Helmut. "Open fire!"

And all hell broke loose.

Drowning in Blood

Successive rapid explosions followed.

With the dark sound of a mighty press-air hammer, the 38 Flak fired hollowly and deadly. In the distance, explosive grenades exploded in a white thunderstorm. The loading dock of the landing craft now approaching to within 600 meters was shredded like paper, and Helmut kept on pushing. *The enemy crews had to squat behind the ramp of their, like sardines in the can. Just fire into the ramps; turn them into mud,* he coached to himself. The men next to him were already pushing the second magazine into the barrel.

The distant smoke confirmed his fiendish work. "Attention, right turn!" shouted Helmut. Not even 400 meters away, the landing craft sloshed uneasily. Helmut whispered, "Lock on target ...fire". He fired_onto the ramp for three seconds. When he was finished, a quarter of the boat seemed to be on fire.

"The third magazine is finished!" shouted Herbert as he loaded the next in a fraction of a second. Herbert was also focused as he reloaded the magazine as easily as he would push a button. Six seconds per magazine was just enough time.

"Hard to the left!" Helmut had sighted the third landing craft. It was swaying so much that he could hardly fix the barrels on the waterline. In the distance, behind the landing craft, the larger ships approaching were now clearly visible. Suddenly, a two-fold, dull bang sounded to the left behind him. Helmut grinned. *About time.* The Eighty-eight on the Flak tower had started shooting.

High explosions appeared on the horizon as a ship's bridge shattered, the glowing iron and debris flying up into the gray sky. The Eighty-eight was a winner. Helmut knew that and smiled.

By now, all of the Eighty-eights had opened fire from their "castle towers," as the soldiers called the Flak towers. Their fire was now calm and precise. They concentrated on the larger ships that were trying to get behind and between the small and fast-landing craft getting closer to the coast.

On his Flakvierling, Helmut continued to aim at the ramps. Out of the corner of his eye, he saw how an Eighty-eight virtually shot the bread off his plate. It fired into the middle of the interior of a large, loaded landing craft. The target was supposed to be his, but he didn't mind. He recognized the marksmanship of the Eighty-eight gunner and saw the whole landing craft go up in flames within seconds. It sank very quickly, surrounded by men struggling in the water.

Again, the Flakvierling swung further to the right. The distance was 300 meters at most. In the ensuing chaos, a boat spun, and the sideline of the ship became clearly visible, an invitation. Four seconds later, pieces of glowing iron flew backward. The landing craft was tilted already, and after a few seconds, the entire page seemed torn open. Helmut fired directly into the open side. The boat was leaning heavily forward into the water, while the ramp was completely shot away. Helmut saw little black figures, survivors from the back part of the boat, crawling over the burning metal walls and then, flopping into the rough sea.

On the right, Helmut saw three or four landing craft that seemed to stop. Their ramps opened, and soldiers amassed for drop-off. The pillow-boxes on the left and right rattled off as the MG gunmen added to the inferno.

"Those are Americans," hissed Herbert while loading the eighth magazine. "You can tell by their helmets."

"Concentrate on the fucking magazine. Attention, swing to the left!"

The Flakvierling 38 produced 180 rounds per minute per barrel, and Helmut saw the penetrating force of the weapon confirmed.

Suddenly, there was a blazing explosion, not 200 meters from the last beach dune, directly in front of Helmut's position. Helmut paused for a few seconds, the smoke blocking his view. Another crackling explosion came, this time just a few hundred meters ahead of him. And then, he saw them coming: frigates, or possibly cruisers—large fighting ships coming closer now with great speed, their medium-caliber artillery firing directly on the Flak positions. "Damn! They want to flatten us!" Helmut spat out.

"Then shouldn't we shoot back?" Herbert asked.

Helmut stayed cool. "Reload. Pivot halfway to the right, now." The four Flak on the left fired dully, targeting the bridge of the cruiser. In the distance flashed smaller explosions. The ship, unimpressed, continued to fire. Helmut shook his head. *What are they doing up in the tower? Are they supposed to stop them all by themselves?"*

"Fire on the cruisers!" came his superior's orders. Helmut would have ignored him if he could. Why was the stupid sergeant always next to his Flak?

Helmut fired on the nearest landing craft, which had almost hit the beach. Six seconds and two magazines later, the front part of the ship was burning from the inside white flares shot skyward, dark lines in between. "Ammo hit!" laughed Herbert, pushing the next magazine in. From behind came the incomprehensible chatter from the sergeant who had probably gone insane. "Dumb and fat go together with him," Helmut quipped to his loading helpers.

"Cruisers on the march!" rang out from behind him and, almost at the same time, came impact explosions. The Eighty-eight on the tower had lowered their barrels and opened fire on the ships. The entire coastline thundered. The Eighty-eight batteries had now zeroed in, and every few hundred meters, all the Flaks fired in rapid succession. Helmut nodded to his comrade. "The boys on the castle towers seem to have finally woken up." Just a few hundred meters from the beach, as if in a chain, there were fiery red explosions, direct hits from an Eighty-eight. Directly beneath the command bridge, a part of a chimney whirled skywards.

"Attention, hard left, craft landed!" Helmut waved the Flakvierling hard to the left, but the angle was too steep; maybe he could still blow off the back of the boat, there was no way to catch the outgoing troops.

"They're getting off!" rang out from the adjacent pillow-box. US soldiers were climbing out man for man with their heavy luggage chest-high into the water. Deafeningly, the MG-42 rattled away from the pillow-box. Helmut could just see a handful of men being shredded down the middle of their bodies. It looked like one only had a part of his body left. Their screams were not heard in the inferno; the figures simply fell forward and sunk.

Helmut shook his head, slightly disgusted. As he swung the Flak back to its upright position, he saw the almost unstoppable masses of landing craft becoming ever thicker. On both sides of his position, some had made it to the beach and had unloaded an army that looked like ants making their way through the water to occupy the beach and key positions. *Not here, not in front of my firing line,* he thought. There was not a single landing craft that had succeeded to set up and disembark in front of Helmut's Flak.

He fired in short intervals alternating between the increasingly thickening attack waves of boats. They seemed endless. But then, the landing craft began to tangle with the boats that had already landed, burning wrecks obstructing the incoming large landing craft. White tracer ammunition from the MGs turned the first waves of the landing craft into a burning and sinking heap of rubble iron.

A dull explosion with gray-white, biting smoke made Helmut pause. He glanced back to the right. Where the Flak tower with the Eighty-eight had just been standing, everything stood still in the dark, black smoke. Through the cloud, he could see only a ruin, like a smoking, collapsed castle tower; the ship's artillery had turned every bit of construction and life into chunks and scrap. Perhaps a kilometer beyond it, Helmut could see the impacts of heavy naval artillery. Everywhere, gigantic blast holes spewed forth in the air. That was no ordinary artillery fire; the mighty barrels of the cruisers and frigates were aiming directly at the Flak towers and bunkers. The earth trembled, the men's eardrums shook, and dark, pungent smoke covered the beaches and dunes where the mightiest forces in the world no longer wanted to permit any life.

Some of the second and third waves of tightly packed landing craft came undamaged onto the beach, and within minutes, GIs were in continental Europe.

Helmut had lost all sense of time, but the loaders warned him that over half of the ammunition had already been used up. Herbert swore. "I think our colleagues 200 meters to the right had three times as much as ammo. We should get over there to grab supplies."

Thomas nodded in agreement. "We need supplies, boss."

Helmut turned the barrels down a few degrees. Now, it was about infantry combat.

"We'll go over there now and get the ammo," Herbert informed the gunner.

"Are you crazy?" screamed Helmut. "Enemy infantry landed right in front of us, and you want to go through the firing line? We'll shoot the rest! There's a troop landing front right. Load, Fire!

Helmut fired the first short burst of explosive projectiles right onto the ramp, where soldiers in rank and file climbed into the water. One could only see smoke and lumps flying up into the air. Then, only scattered figures jumped into the water. A man's arm was shot off. He limped a few feet onto the ramp and then, twitched like a dancer who was under the influence of drugs. An MG burst of fire had caught him and sent him to heaven.

Smoke came out from the pillow-boxes, and the MG barrels glowed almost red-hot. Out of the corner of his eye, Helmut saw the crews desperately trying to exchange the overheated barrels. The neighboring MG fired helpfully_into the resulting gap. The soldiers fired directly at the mass of enemy soldiers, who somehow, despite murderous counter-fire, stalked in small groups ever closer and closer to the defensive positions. There were a few knocks on the Flak shield a couple of times. The Americans were firing rifle fire at the Flak, trying to hit the crew. Now, it was getting serious.

"Men, get the Schmeisser out!" Helmut shouted at his loaders. "They want to bust us, so now, it's do or die!"

The men knew what to do. Herbert and Thomas each took a Schmeisser MP out of the box, preloaded with a magazine. "One for everyone, and that's it" gasped Herbert.

Thomas looked puzzled at the black MP. "These things can only be fired fully automatic?" The words were barely out of his mouth when another burst of fire hailed down against their protective shield. "Why are you talking?" shouted Helmut. "Shoot them down, the dogs."

Clumsily, Thomas peeked out the side of the shield to catch a glimpse of the enemy and started firing. He shot wildly and nervously around. Helmut saw from his seat that a whole group of enemy soldiers had approached the Flak almost unnoticed. The enemy had targeted his Flak, focusing in on him. He cursed mentally. "Give me that thing!" he snapped at Thomas. Helmut grabbed the Schmeissers, set himself up on his seat, and fired directly above the shield into the enemy soldiers who were lurking behind a dune. Most of them fell like bowling pins.

The heavy MG rattled from inside the pillow-box. And from the larger box lying to the left, at least two Mgs now fired at the same time. Still, it looked as though enemy troops had settled somewhere up at the front. There, right in front of Helmut's position, not a hundred meters from him on the beach, the enemy had entrenched themselves. The MG burst of fire rushed straight through the dunes to their position. Sand blasts sprayed everywhere and, from time to time, dark pieces flew through the air. Suddenly, he saw balls fly through the air, and explosions went off at the front of the beach. The enemy had come so close that some of Helmut's comrades were already fighting with hand grenades. Shots in the direction of the Flak fell silent, and Helmut knew that the soldiers in the pillow-boxes were good throwers.

Just ahead of Helmut's section, a new bundle of landing craft came closer, twice the size of the first wave. Helmut, guided by instinct, screamed at the men, "Load the explosive grenades! Ready?" Two seconds later, he had the first giant ramp in his crosshairs. "Fire," whispered Helmut. Nothing happened. He pressed the lever. No fire "It's jammed!" Helmut screamed. "Magazines out. Reload, fast!"

"Already done; now, go!" Herbert snorted back. Again nothing. But they heard a loud humming, and in that moment, they knew what had arrived: low-flying fighter-bombers. They had been waiting for them. Rive, aircraft turned in a curve and were barely 30 meters over the beach as they raced behind each other toward the Flak position. "Take cover! Down!" shouted Helmut.

Nothing happened for about two seconds. Then, all hell broke loose as bombs rained down on their position. They heard four bursting explosions 30 meters further to the right and then, exactly one explosion above the pillow-box. Concrete pieces and smoke mingled together to form a dark hot gas cloud. Helmut thought he was suffocating. Someone shouted, but the two loaders stood like pillars, unperturbed and uninjured on the magazine shaft. "They'll be back!" shouted Herbert. "Hey, there's a big fat pot rolling toward us over there!"

A very large landing craft approach several hundred meters away, and as it lowered its ramp, Helmut saw a Sherman tank come out and roll down into the shallows.

"Panzer!" Helmut shouted to his comrades. They had lost several important seconds due to the air raid and the jam, seconds that the enemy was using to land a few dozen panzers. Black monsters came through the swirling cloud of smoke on the beach, one after the other. The loading ramps of the ships rolled down, landing in the middle of Helmut's section. Helmut cursed inwardly. *Don't we have some PAKs behind us standing by somewhere? Where is the fucking Luftwaffe?*

Desperately, the men tried to exchange the magazines. In, out. The load lever and cartridge had to be withdrawn and reset. "Still jamming. Shit!" commented Helmut. He almost choked on his words because, at the same time, to the left and to the right, the familiar small explosions went off. The neighboring Flaks opened fire almost simultaneously with explosive grenades, directly on the disembarking Shermans.

The Shermans were flaring up. Glowing pieces of metal spewed out from the chains of the first panzer. The second received a direct hit from the Eighty-eight, and another one was out of luck. Flak bursts of fire caught the Sherman from the side; the engine immediately caught fire and, seconds later, the rear end of the panzer was red from explosions. A few projectiles had apparently let motor oil and ammunition merge.

"Men, either we get this thing going, or we'll break, get it?" Desperately, Helmut pushed the box to the back, and suddenly, a damaged, unexploded cartridge popped out. Helmut moved into position, and in a fraction of a second, fired the Flakvierling. Hits! But the Sherman's slanted front armor deflected his projectiles into the sky, and the panzer just kept going, adjusting its position, the cannon barrel now aimed straight at the Flak position.

Helmut's crew cursed. He couldn't normally crack a Sherman with a Flak, but he had no choice. He fired. The 20-mm projectiles bounced off, and the Sherman rushed full-throttle towards the Flak, the cannon barrel of the panzer aimed directly at them.

Helmut shouted, "Down, cover, down!" Helmut did not hear his own words. He could only feel how he slammed into the sand after a wild leap. Fire and explosion followed. Helmut turned like a snake in the sand crawling on all fours, moving himself meter by meter away from the Flak. The explosion was dull, a bright bursting sound; he sensed a close and glistening light and then, smoke, he was surrounded by black smoke. He felt his legs; his body was intact.

Then, he turned and saw the Flak wrapped in smoke, and amidst the rubble lay men looking like charred sacks. Helmut tried to struggle to his feet, but he lacked the strength, and maybe the will, too shocked to move. He recognized Herbert, his smoking corpse laying directly in front of him. A few meters ahead lay Thomas, unmistakably dead. Helmut felt an infinite emptiness, and dropped his head to the sand.

A nearby explosion brought him to his senses. He knew he had to survive, here and now. He shuffled back to the pillow-box. Its concrete walls promised some protection from the inferno.

Feeling safer behind the wall, Helmut took in the scene more thoroughly. He noticed that the upper part of his boot was missing. Blood was dripping from the open spot. "Shrapnel!" he cursed; a piece of metal had destroyed his boot and had caused a bleeding flesh wound. But Helmut knew that it was only a superficial wound that looked worse than it was.

He continued crawling right behind the half-destroyed pillow-box, and suddenly, he fell back, flopping back into something soft. Startled and disgusted, he turned around and stared in disbelief at a kind of pressed-in football, a yellow-red blood clot that looked strange. Apparently, an enemy MG burst of fire had shaved off the front half of the man's face. Nose, chin, and cheeks were simply blown away, but the bushy eyebrows still stuck to the forehead. Without any doubt, here lay the fat, stupid sergeant, or rather what was left of him. Next to the dead, there was a leather shoulder bag. Helmut grabbed the dead man's bag. *Schnapps and maps, I hope. Officers always have something useful with them,* he thought cheerfully.

Helmut crept further to the back of the bunker, where he finally found cover in a sandpit beside a bunker wall. Breathing heavily, he looked around the corner. There, on the beach, the inferno was raging in full force; barely a hundred meters ahead, many enemy soldiers seemed to have found cover behind some rubble. They were firing sporadically at the German MG positions, aiming again and again at the embrasures of the pillow-boxes.

Looking right into the distance, Helmut could make out a group of panzers and trucks that were practically swinging around on the beach, almost undisturbed. Perhaps the enemy was luckier over there? At sea, more waves of landing craft tried to sail around the wreckage of the first landing wave, but the still existing Flakvierlings gave them hell. They tore up the metal walls and shot the occupants to pieces. Directly in front of his section, a landing craft was in the water. It seemed capsized now; from within its tilted position, countless bodies could be seen. It looked unnatural, dark parts sloshing in dark liquid, as if the soldiers were drowned in their own blood.

Helmut looked behind him. Any second, enemy soldiers could appear who would try to attack the bunker from behind. Inland, in the background, he glimpsed at several half-blown up, still smoking castle towers; as far as he could see, all the Eighty-eights on the Flak towers seemed to have been neutralized.

Helmut had just taken cover behind the dune when he heard voices. "Just lie down, and we'll get you out." Helmut was astonished when he recognized the crouching figures as paramedics. There four of them, two of whom carried a seriously wounded man on a stretcher. A very young paramedic approached Helmut and said, "Stay down; we'll patch you up. Do you need morphine?"

"It's not so bad. I can go, I think."

"Well, you come with us; it's over for you. Just get out of here!"

Reluctantly, Helmut picked himself up. Not even 50 meters behind the dunes, two Red Cross trucks and paramedics were fully occupied with the treatment of the wounded.

The young man helped Helmut to the truck.

"Sit down in the front. Let's go."

But no sooner had they driven off than Helmut heard a deadly noise. The familiar humming could not be ignored. Helmut tried to see the aircraft from the side windows. "Damn it! We're getting visitors from above!"

The driver swore and made a full stop. "Everyone out! Take cover where you can!"

The men sprang in panic from the truck and ran in all directions.

Helmut was barely out of the truck when he saw how the planes had lined up behind each other in a steep curve. "Those are fighter-bombers. They're going to attack!"

"I don't understand," said the driver "that would be against the Geneva Conventions."

"Cover!" Helmut interrupted. "They don't recognize us as the Red Cross. Everyone, get away from the street! Find a ditch or stand behind a tree."

The paramedics were running, but there was no time for the wounded in the truck.

"Run!" He yelled at a teenaged paramedic standing rooted to the middle of the road.

D-DAY REPULSED

Fighter Bombers

The men dove into the ditches, which were no more than shallow holes, not deep enough to safely escape death or injury.

Like clockwork, the fighters came thundering down. In seconds, their fire would catch the trucks from the side. Helmut crouched as far as he could into the ditch. After the flashes came the well-known murderous rattle of the aircraft cannons. Helmut crouched deeper and, seconds later, he felt the air pressure of the successive explosions; the air was full of bursting and glowing metal pieces that were flying like fireballs over the trenches. Out of the corner of his eye, he saw a comrade with a glowing metal rod through his chest. He collapsed backward, his jacket a half-charred lump.

The machine gun fire fell silent. Cautiously, he raised his head a few centimeters higher and saw the aircraft turn around in a high arc. The Red Cross trucks were burning like torches. Suddenly, a violent explosion threw Helmut onto the asphalt. A nearby ammunition vehicle must have exploded. Everywhere, small and big fires, intervening cries, and black smoke made the chaos complete.

Helmut got up. Burning, charred remains lay scattered in the street. Now, Helmut recognized that there were other burning trucks to the left and right of the road. There were also half-track vehicles, ammunition transports; the aircraft had focused on those. The moan behind him turned his attention back to the paramedics. Miraculously, a few men seemed to be as uninjured as he was.

The paramedics supported each other, the small group limping along the roadside. Helmut helped a severely wounded man, who was missing his lower leg and, in full consciousness, was trying to move forward as best he could.

"We aren't even five kilometers from the coast. If they break through, they'll get us," Helmut noted.

"And? We're paramedics," said the young man who had helped into the truck, "and they're not Russians, after all."

"Maybe the enemy pilot who shot at us was of a different opinion. They confused us with the ammunition trucks."

The young man shook his head in disbelief. "Then, we won't get out of here."

"Where is the medical center?"

"Behind Bayeux. Help me get out of here."

Helmut shook his head. "It's too far. Best get back to the bunkers on the beach. We'll have cover there, and medical attention."

"Let's support each other; come, men! There's a crossroads with trees up ahead. With any luck, maybe some Wehrmacht vehicles will pass by."

Silently, the small pitiful group made their way up the road. It was only a few minutes later when the comrades could hardly believe their luck. "Attention, there are vehicles coming in front," the paramedic spat out. "And behind it a panzer? I don't believe it!"

"Panzer?" asked Helmut. "At best, it's the reconnaissance brigade of a division. The panzer divisions are deep in the hinterland, as far as I know."

Helmut recognized a Horch 901, a Kuebelwagen, and a single panzer. The column approached and slowed down. Helmut could see from the rank and file sitting on the vehicles that he was right about his assumption. And he saw something even more surprising. The soldiers had camouflage covers over their helmets. Only the SS did that. The Kuebelwagen stopped next to the limping men.

"Behave yourselves, guys," whispered Helmut to his paramedic comrades. "They want information. As long as they're not drunk, we won't have any problems."

Helmut recognized the mistrust in the eyes of the mostly very young SS rascals. For a fraction of a second, he wondered if he should make a joke saying they looked as if they were still sleeping in bed with Mama. But he did not want to bet on the humor of the SS. For Helmut, it was clear that this was just an advance column of the SS Division Hitler Youth which, as far as he could remember, should be just to the right of Caen. A few of the SS boys went about getting their machine gun ready; of course, the SS had only the best, sometimes even in abundance, but as Helmut knew, there was nothing free in life. Everything had its price, and the HJ division would pay with their blood.

The Unterscharfuehrer looked around nervously for aircraft and then, walked directly to Helmut.

"You've been bombed?"

"It looks that way," Helmut answered with a playful nonchalance, knowing that with encounters with the SS, you never knew.

The Unterscharfuehrer walked around Helmut, hand on holster. "Show your wound."

Helmut pulled up his blood-soaked trouser leg.

"You call that an injury? You want to be transported away?"

"I'm from the Flak. The paramedics picked me up right on the beach under enemy fire."

"I don't care!" For a few seemingly eternal seconds, the SS officer stared at Helmut's tired eyes.

The paramedics stood around Helmut. "Can you take us with you?" one of them asked innocently.

The officer held a hand to the opened pistol holster. Unexpectedly, he craned his head up, checking the sky for aircraft. "All right, mount," ordered the officer.

Helmut was allowed to sit on a half-track manned by the SS without any further threat.

"Well, guys" grinned the young SS man, "where are you coming from now? Did you see any fighter-bombers?"

Helmut nodded. "They could come back at any minute."

The teenaged soldier turned to the sergeant. "We've had good luck so far. Further to the north, there were apparently some dramatics."

The SS officer twitched with a half-smile. "Dramatics? They almost killed us!"

"Fighter bombers?" Helmut asked.

"Those too, but directly above our division, heavy bombers unloaded. Thousands of explosives and incendiary bombs. To the east of Caen, the villages are burning, but they were coming after us!"

Helmut nodded, concerned. "This isn't a decoy. This is a proper invasion."

"And it's happening right here, I can tell you that."

"Losses?"

The Unterscharfuehrer's gaze darkened. "Sure. What else do you want to know?"

Helmut did not want to say or ask anything more. But he could see how the SS boys dispensed cigarettes. But they seemed disciplined, even made a motivated impression. Helmut had "the pleasure" of meeting SS soldiers several times. They were young soldiers and real professionals; their attitude was ice-cold, and they carried their weapons as if they could start combat at any second. Somehow, despite their young age, they had exuded confidence, and Helmut could sense it. *This officer is an asshole, but anyway, these SS guys gave compassion to the wounded. They're an example to my other comrades from the Flak unit,* Helmut thought.

"Hey!" snapped the SS officer to Helmut. "We lost radio contact. Do you have a good map?"

Helmut pulled out a small field division map from his shoulder bag and unfurled it.

"Here," he pointed. "We are right on the border between the command fronts of the 15th and 7th Army."

"Good map, young man. I could make good use of it," said the SS man half-smugly.

"Well, strictly speaking, we are also on the border of the commanders," replied Helmut.

Smiling, the Unterscharfuehrer lit up a cigarette. "We have nothing to do with that, boy. We only have one commander who comes from the top. And I'm not talking about God here, all right?"

Helmut looked at him incredulously.

At that moment, he heard the familiar noise again.

"Fighter bombers! Aircraft, approaching from the left!" shouted the driver in the Kuebelwagen as he jumped out and ran into the middle of the main street.

The SS officer shouted, "Go fast, you idiots. Go for that group of trees!" All the men leaped off the vehicles like dogs, seeking shelter behind trees and bushes on the roadside.

The humming was mighty close. Helmut looked up and saw a couple of the American Thunderbolts that he had heard of. They had rockets, and the planes were supposed to be hard to take down even with Flak. The fighter-bombers now clearly turned towards the column. They had been seen them and, at least, the fate of the vehicles was clear.

Seconds later, Helmut saw the Horch and Kuebelwagen bursting into fiery pieces. Only the panzer seemed to be moving forward. It did not concern Helmut. He turned back toward his comrades. Supporting each other, the group hobbled back toward the beach.

"We are only a few kilometers from the coast. I can see the fortress bunker from here."

"We can do it," gasped the comrade.

They were probably not a hundred meters from the protective bunker when Helmut flinched and pulled his comrade by the shoulder behind a tree. "Away from the road." In fact, as if from an unreal film, figures recognizable by their green uniforms set out to surround the bunker from behind and besiege it. "Enemy parachute troops. What do you have with you?"

"Nothing at all. We paramedics aren't armed."

Helmut shook his head in disbelief. He opened his pistol holster and pulled out a Belgian 9mm Browning, his souvenir from the glory days. "Attention, there are soldiers approaching us ahead."

Somewhere in front of the bunker, there were shots being fired. It seemed the bunker crew was trying to keep the enemy paratroopers from the entrances.

"Hey!" screamed his comrade. "There are some coming with their bayonets fixed."

"Get ready. It looks as if they landed in large numbers nearby. There are more ahead."

"How do we get to the bunker?"

"We sneak off the road and get to the bunker from the back. Avoid enemy contact where it's possible."

Only a few meters from the bunker, the small group hid behind a dune. What they saw filled the men with utter dismay.

They were probably the fastest and most disgusting seconds of his life—real hand-to-hand combat, dark survival in the death zone around the bunker.

The ferocity of that fighting astonished the men. In the near distance, soldiers were lunging at each other with fixed bayonets and with their rifle stocks, and Helmut could even recognize some men with entrenching tools or shovels. The enemy was charging upon the gunners in the barbed wire entanglements up there. Some men were in flames, and other men were shooting or stabbing them as they staggered. Helmut could no longer see which men were from which army, as the smoke and flames made them all a similar outline as they fought.

In the dim light around the corner, he saw the enemy. The American stabbed one German to death through his abdomen with a bayonet and then threw him like a sack to the side. Not a second later, the same soldier had already finished off a second German. He had forced his bayonet directly through the neck of the man. It came clearing out the back with blood spraying out. A German soldier ran toward the fighting soldier with a spade, hitting the man full in the face. Both fell to the ground, and Helmut could hardly believe what he saw: the German wrestled the soldier's gun out of his hand, jumped back, and shot him in the chest. But he didn't die immediately, so the German gave him a second shot, and, at the same time, stabbed the bayonet into the enemy soldier. The German had only won briefly, though, as more and more whistling shots rang out. Helmut ducked, and when he looked up briefly, he saw how his countryman had fallen, hit by a bullet.

There were shots everywhere. Suddenly, a thick brown uniform with a helmet appeared less than 10 meters from Helmut's cover. The man had not yet seen Helmut's position. He brandished an assault rifle, most likely looking for the back entrance to the bunker; the fat soldier only looked at the bunker and seemed to have no sense of his surroundings. Helmut got up, aimed at his face and pulled the trigger.

Explosions created dull, little clouds of smoke in the immediate vicinity. "Grenade launchers! From our own people. They don't know we're here too. To the bunker!" Another man to his right was hit by shrapnel in the head under his helmet, and his skull was completely opened up above one ear, with his brain matter visible.

"There is the iron door! Our boys have managed to free up the entrance again!"

Helmut nudged his comrade and, crouching, they crept to the iron back door of the locked bunker.

Helmut felt how his strength was slowly subsiding, but rest was unthinkable right now. "I don't see any more paratroopers. We have to make ourselves known to the boys inside."

"Are you sure they'll let us in?"

"As long as they don't think we're enemy soldiers; we can do it."

Helmut could hear German voices coming from inside the bunker. He scrambled to his feet, leaning close to the concrete wall, the hatch beside his head. "Hey, are you okay there? Let me in; do you hear?"

"Password?" It echoed from the inside.

"Forget your password!" scolded Helmut back. "I'm a Grenadier from the Flak. We lost our position, and I'm standing here with my arse in the fire! Open up!"

The hatch opened a few centimeters, Helmut looked into the barrel of an MP-40. After a few long seconds, the steel hatch opened and an older soldier with an iron cross around his neck waved him in.

The interior of the bunker reminded Helmut of his study trip to Rome, when he visited the old church catacombs with centuries-old muff and dust. The concrete and the floating smoke smelled the same way. Everything was in the semi-dark, with barely enough air to breathe.

At the front of the embrasure were two MGs, One was unoccupied. In front of it was a hunched body; even from a few meters away, Helmut could see the man had been shot in the neck. A bullet had smashed smoothly through it.

Next to him, the load gunner groaned. He must have been on the receiving end of something bad; his face and hair were dark red, smeared with blood, but he was trying to push the ammunition belt back into the MG. The man was brave. He knew there was no time to worry about his injuries.

The gunman in the rear embrasure fired almost continuously. The MG-42 was positioned at the embrasure, a concrete slit about one meter wide at head height, and the gunner was standing on a platform to work the gun. Two men were already there, talking in an agitated way, manning the gun.

Helmut jumped onto the platform. The loader, who, despite his facial injury, looked at least as cool and focused as Helmut's men had been before.

The veteran shoved a stool toward Helmut and threw him a cigarette. "You come from the Flak? How did they get you?"

"The first tanks that came through landed in front of my section. My gun was hit directly."

The old man nodded, lighting a fag for himself. "What's the situation out there? Has the enemy taken up position to our left?"

Helmut drew the smoke in deeply, shaking his head. "Not really. A few groups have settled in front of the waterline and some others behind the dunes."

The MG fell silent for a few seconds. "Attention, aircraft ahead!" roared the gunner. Helmut caught a glimpse through the gap. The planes made three small, black dots in the sky; their dropped bombs flew very fast, heading straight for the bunker and the open slits.

"Take cover!" Direct impacts made the vault tremble as thick concrete chunks flew from the ceiling. The pressure squeezed the air out of the men's lungs, and the hot dust pressed like a mantle of death on everything that still lived.

The pressure of the next explosion hurled Helmut onto the concrete wall. Sharp smoke was everywhere and then, light. Helmut blinked, looking upward through a huge hole in the concrete ceiling. The smoke was sucked out as if through a chimney.

Then, everything was calm again, except for the dust that still hung everywhere and the crackling sound of burning material. Helmut wiped the dust from his face. The MG gunman was still sitting under the embrasure, looking like a black sack and barely recognizable; a piece of concrete splitting his skull open with a hole as wide as a hand above his ear from which a reddish mass bubbled out. Helmut knew it was the man's brain, or whatever was left of it.

Coughing, a few men stood up. The old man stumbled in the direction of the embrasure. "Come on, help me, put him to the side." Helmut staggered forward. There were rubble and concrete everywhere. Without hesitating, he pushed the corpse aside and knelt facing the MG, checking the direction and ammunition. A young puppy-faced soldier struggled closer in the silence and, without being asked, took the cartridge belt and shoved it into the shaft. Helmut unlocked it and looked through the front and rear sights.

"All men to their posts! Go on!" shouted the old man.

Helmut searched intently for the ramps of the fresh landing craft. Who knew how many waves the enemy was sending? His head was bright red from the stress, and he felt a deep first thirst coming on. He breathed briefly and deeply. He had to try to concentrate. Up ahead on the water, the ships rocked, the nearest landing craft less than 300 meters away. As ordered, they dumped their ramps onto the surf. "Done," he whispered to the loading helper. The man just muttered something, probably a vague yes. *He seems to have gotten injured, too. But no time to think about that. As long as he can load, we'll keep going.*

Let them get out, Helmut advised himself. The shadows of American soldiers jumped into the water. Slowly, one after the other, they advanced toward him into the shallower water. The waves came up to their chests, then their waists. Helmut pressed his rifle butt tightly into his shoulder and squeezed the trigger. The MG thundered away, a mighty weapon. He mowed the fire straight into the middle of the figures; from a distance, he saw bodies going up and down as if performing a kind of dance. He hit most of them just above the waterline, at belly-height. Helmut corrected; he wanted to hit the guys at chest level. Then, they would sink faster with their luggage and free up the view of the men behind them so he could shred the next row.

MGs thundered down the entire coastal section, along with some small-caliber Flaks still capable of firing before they were destroyed or ran out of ammunition. Not a single Eighty-eight could be heard. Suddenly, a threatening, now more familiar sound could be heard: the increasingly louder noise of the propellers of fast approaching fighter-bombers. Somehow, for a fraction of a second, Helmut hoped for the Luftwaffe, but it was an illusion. Not a single German plane had been seen in the last few hours.

Alert and slightly nervous, Helmut peered up through the concrete slit and saw a horizontal line of three aircraft descending on the beach at great speed. These planes had very large radial engines, which from former training and recognition sessions, he knew was distinctive of the Thunderbolt plane. They seemed to pick up speed the closer they came. They flew in low at maybe 30 meters.

"Flak! Where is the flak behind us?" Helmut barely uttered the last word as a familiar sound hammered outside. Somewhere behind the bunker, an intact 20-mm Flak was still in position firing at the first fighter-bombers; the tracer ammunition seemed to fire exactly at the cockpit, without effect, and yet, a fireball exploded in the air. A hit, 200 meters away from the bunker!

The plane, with half a wing engulfed in a ball of fire, struck the quarries in front of the bunker with a flash; spitting loudly, huge parts flying in all directions. Helmut could feel the heat through the open embrasures, and he thought he saw that somewhere over the whirl of fire, a dark doll flew skywards.

The milksop-faced man behind him held his head in his hands for a moment. This was virtually the losing of his virginity, the first real explosions on his doorstep.

Helmut took out his binoculars. "Stay on the ammo belt, boy; more aircraft approaching." Helmut himself knew his words were empty. MGs against Thunderbolts? *Nothing we can do here will stop them.* And they came thundering down on a steep descent before turning in toward the bunker and leveling out at a low altitude with sparks flying from the underside of their wings "Damn! They're firing rockets. Heads down!" Helmut shouted. He knew it was going to get hot and hellish.

The men jumped into each corner, crouching and pressing their helmets over their heads.

They Turn Away

The emergency ventilation finally seemed to work as the clouds of smoke in the bunker became lighter. Helmut could finally open his eyes again, but he didn't know if he wanted to. They were burning from the smoke. He heard crackling and clattering everywhere, but otherwise, it had become quieter. There was occasional short machine gun fire, but hardly any cannon fire, and the intervals between the explosions became longer. What had happened?

Helmut lifted the binoculars, inspecting the beach. The clouds of smoke also seemed to have cleared over the water. But the smoking debris of the half-sunk and destroyed landing craft could not be ignored. Helmut handed the glasses to the loader. "The boats..." Helmut pointed with his hand straight at the water. "You see, the boats seem to have stopped."

"Strange. There's something wrong," the loader replied sheepishly. "It looks as if the landing craft are coming to a halt 500 meters from the shoreline."

"Left!. Look to the left" interrupted Helmut excitedly. "There, you see; they're turning around. Ten, 15 boats seem to be maneuvering backward."

"It looks weird, but when they turn sideways, the Eighty-eights will nab them with a coup de grace."

Helmut could not resist a grin. "*The* coup de grace, as they say here in France..." A distant but enormous explosion destroyed the entertaining silence. "Hey, you see?" Helmut clenched a joyful fist.

"Over there, they attempted to turn sideways and were hit right in the side by our artillery."

"Split into two pieces," the loader happily interjected. In the meantime, everybody that was left unscathed dragged themselves to the firing slit to intently watch the unfolding drama. "Guys, they're turning back!"

"Best to be at your positions. They can still turn around. More plane attacks are possible at any second …"

"We have a radio message from Gustav Bunker," interrupted the old man. "Enemy paratroopers are trying to penetrate there. They're throwing fire grenades into the shafts."

The bunker officer limped to the embrasures. "Didn't you hear? To your positions! That can happen to us too. The poor pigs over there probably have more burnt human flesh than we do."

The loader could barely hide his enthusiasm. "Man, look at the waves!"

Helmut shook his head. "Barely any waves. The water suddenly seems to be flat, like a mirror."

"No, no. The color," interjected the loader. "The little waves, the water."

Helmut nodded. "Red, dark red, recognizable even from here."

"How many did we get, do you think?"

Helmut reached for the binoculars again. "In front of our section, here, 500 are swimming belly up in the water, maybe more."

The loader nodded in surprise as the officer approached behind him. "Guys, we have news. There's an urgent need for a rear Flak Unit. It comes directly from the Reserve Officer."

Helmut turned around, confused. "Me? Is that supposed to be a joke? They can turn around any second."

"It doesn't look that way. I can't believe it. We forced them to turn around, but we just got word that five miles to our left, our boys are in trouble. The ships' artillery plowed everything over there. I have orders to ask for support from the Flak."

"We're busy," answered Helmut hesitantly.

"You have to help them. A whole train of Flak, all Flakvierlings, is fixed 500 meters behind us. The crew has suffered heavy casualties."

"Let me stay here." Helmut pointed to his dark red, blood-soaked boot.

The old man smiled at him. "That's nothing. But you've done a lot here, young man. I guarantee that will be noted. But you're one of the Flak guys, so..."

Helmut felt his strength start to fade. Nevertheless, he picked himself up and left the bunker without another word.

The road to the coastline was a route he did not know personally; it was an earth and sand track, interrupted by old cobblestone parts, suitable for farm tractors, not for tanks. But it was partially sunken below ground level, which reminded him more of deep Russia than Europe, and it was screened to the north and west by a thick hedgerow of the type the French called 'bocage. But in all the chaos and destruction, even walking short distances took its toll. In reality, the positions were separated only by a few hundred meters. At the end of the street, he finally saw the large, unfinished bunker. Next to it, in the protection of the concrete walls were still two Flak Units, both on half-track vehicles. Soldiers flailed around the cannon. *They seem to have a problem*, Helmut thought.

"I'm glad you came," said a young officer. "Our gunners are dead, and all our barrels are jammed."

Helmut swung himself up onto a Flakvierling. "Let's see what we can do."

The young soldiers looked unsure. They had to get the Flak ready before the next fighter-bombers arrived. Barely a moment later, they heard the drone of engines straight ahead. "Panzer?" one of them asked, startled.

Helmut shook his head in disbelief. *What else do they want to throw at us? Ship's artillery, panzers, landing craft, bombers?* "Alright. Get ready. We have to be ready to fire, even if all the barrels aren't ready."

In the distance, he heard explosions, mighty impacts. Ships' artillery again.

But it was a short-lived interlude. And the explosions were less frequent here.

The officer remained calm, searching the area with his binoculars. "Two panzers are burning on the beach. No more panzers visible."

"It's going to get dark soon. Maybe we should dig trenches," Helmut suggested. He was tired and wouldn't be able to stand much longer.

"Yes. And when it gets dark, take cover. But rest now."

Those were magic words, and not for Helmut only. Instinctively, he knew he had survived for today. Had he kept his honor? He believed so, but only God knew for sure. He let himself fall on sandbags and noticed that his comrades were already doing the same. He was about to nod off in exhaustion, though he still felt his pulse racing. The longest day was coming to an end.

Debarkation

Why did the man behind me have to throw up on my back? Walter thought. He looked at his comrades who seemed stuffed in a can and left to their fate. Admittedly, it was tight in the landing craft, and the otherwise boisterous buddies were more serious than Faust. Not one tried to crack stupid jokes. *The roaring sound of the engine, the nasty smell of diesel fumes, and this rocking movement are all we get now.*

"Get up! Stand in line!" came the order from the sergeant.

The soldiers awkwardly rose with their heavy backpacks and M1 rifles.

"Close ranks!"

One soldier after another struggled to hold his stance with one hand on the shoulder of the man in front of him in a four-man chain. Walter chuckled, knowing that if one man fell, everyone fell. He grinned at his neighbor, who only stared blankly ahead, his chest full of puke and looking like death already.

Suddenly, the ramp opened, and Walter saw small flashes everywhere, followed by rapid explosions, almost like firecrackers, then a lightning-like force ran into his ear. In the delusion of pain, he tore the backpack from the shoulder of the man in front of him.

Suddenly, there was a splintering and crackling sound that reminded him of bursting shards of glass. When Walter heard a thick whistle close to his face, he instinctively knew that he was in trouble. And within a fraction of a second, he felt a sting in his ear, deep and hot. At the same time, something hard pressed against his shoulder. He was pushed to the ground.

"Down!" he heard the man behind him yell. Walter held his hand on his now terribly aching ear, blood flowing in streams down his hand and arm. "Your ear." he heard his comrade say. "They shot your ear off. Get out. Get off the ship, fast!"

Next, Walter felt a rough jab in his lower back. Seconds later, he slammed into the water, and immediately, the heavy rucksack and rifle pushed him down. He wanted to scream, but the cold, salty water stopped up his throat. Somehow, he came up again. His arms paddled in panic. His feet couldn't find the ground.

His pulse raced. Under his foot, he finally found purchase, and with all his might, he pushed his body upward. He tried swimming motions, but the backpack pushed him further downward, like the devil trying to hold him in Hell. With a jerky motion, he tore the pack off his body and was free at last.

Beside him in the water, something dark and round sloshed. A soldier, his helmet slipping backward, gasped, slamming his arms into the water. Suddenly, the man jerked his head in Walter's direction, almost touching him, and Walter stared, his head had turned dark red in a split second; the back of the man's head spat out a yellow-red, slimy mass into the water; lifeless and quietly disturbed eyes of the dead stared at him. Walter heard himself gasping, then thought, *Forward, only forward, out of the water.*

In front of him, men swam or waded along, fighting their way through the waves. Metal pillars seemed to stick out of the waves everywhere. Walter clung to one of the poles, panting hard, trying to catch his breath. His eyes burned. He held onto the pole with one hand, and with the other, wiped the sea salt from his eyes. He caught a glimpse of his hand, seemingly covered in red paint. He could still feel the throbbing and burning where shreds of his left ear still hung. He felt his heavy breathing. He was still alive, but he did not want to—could not—go on. *Just breathe. Rest. Keep the water out of my lungs.*

Thick smoke wafted over the water, obscuring the view ahead, where men lay on the beach, seemingly hiding for hours. Walter had his legs wrapped around the iron pole, ice cold railroad tracks mounted crosswise, he recognized now. His breath was calm, but the cold the waves that were not getting calmer engulfed his bones, or so he believed. Over and over again, bursts of fire from MGs or chain-like blasts from small-caliber cannons fired to the left and right.

All kinds of things were swimming beside or in front of him in the water. For a few seconds, he saw only legs floating by with a few remnants of belt and stomach. *Not here, not now. You have to make it.*

With only carnage and water around him, he wondered, *Does God exist? Should I pray? This might be a good time to start.* But then, blasts of water sprayed just a few feet away from him. He could see a landing craft that had been hit from the side completely covered in smoke, leaning slowly sideways, and somewhere on shore, a cannon was trying to apply the coup de grace. Even though Walter's body was shaking, he could feel the heat of the burning wreck on his face.

He could feel the cold water rising up to his waist, but he knew that he had to hold out where he was. The beach was littered with corpses and dying men; if he went forward now, it wouldn't be long before the Germans would find him. And after that, only darkness would follow.

A few meters away, the bulky iron poles towered above him. They were dark spears, crossed metal rails, and most of them were mounted with mines. Some were much thicker than others. Directly next to them, a piece of wreckage protruded out of the water. It looked like a metal box where he could take cover. Meter by meter, he dragged himself toward the metal container; and as soon as he had a firm grip, dizziness seized him. His adrenaline level tanked, and his ear began to burn furiously.

Slowly, the cold wind stirred his senses, and he could almost think again. But time seemed to stand still. *So stupid. Such a fool,* Walter thought. Then, the waves grew stronger again. He felt his legs cramping and knew that he would not be able to hold on for long. The container wobbled, and he slid deeper. He couldn't feel the ground. Slowly, his hands parted from the cold metal. He leaned back into the water and let his body float on the waves. Darkness. Minutes and hours did not matter.

When Walter came back to his senses, the first thing he felt was the cold. And sand. *Low tide. It's already night.* He lied in wait on the beach. Somehow, with God's help, he had washed ashore, and everything around him had calmed down. His senses seemed clear again.

The black shadow, three meters beside him, was recognizable without a helmet: a corpse. Fortunately, everything was still fresh. Walter always thought corpses would stink like rotten chicken, but now, it was clear it had something to do with decay, not the simple state of being dead. The comrade had probably been shot down only six or seven hours beforehand. The man's head looked like a dented football. It was clear that a projectile, from probably a heavy machine gun, had cut half his head clean off.

Then, voices. Were they comrades? He sensed he was in an isolated, desperate position. He thought his company was a few hundred meters away in the dunes behind the beach, where there was still shooting.

He also heard a few explosions. *Hand grenades?* The Germans were skilled at throwing stalk hand grenades. Their every throw meant shredded meat. Walter did not want that, not such an end. And he knew that if he stayed where he was, he didn't have a chance. But where to go? Ahead was a half sunken landing craft. But it was at least 200 meters away. He probably wouldn't be seen in the dark, but he had a bad feeling. The boat already looked half-capsized. So far, he had been lucky, but he felt a squeeze in his stomach. Fear. It could be all over today.

A few hundred meters in front of him, half in the now-flat surf, stood some Rommelspargel protruding like ghostly fences out from the water. *Metal is good cover*. Behind a lean post, Walter ducked to avoid being caught by any snipers. His cover was more than adequate. He trembled slightly, the cool wind and wetness paralyzing his limbs, but he had to hold out. He had to last until dawn.

The Barn

Helmut was at the end of his tether. "Don't fall asleep, young man!" yelled the officer behind him. "We have to get out of here right away."

"Out of here? Where to?"

"Ahead on the beach, snipers could lie in wait. Some are hiding behind the barriers. And apart from that, we also have to get a free line of fire. They can come back at any time… And there are still thousands of ships lurking out there."

"We should wait until tomorrow. If we run out there now, and there are snipers..."

"Take it easy," interrupted the officer. "We'll go when it's dark. You can rest for a few beats, but don't sleep. Understood?"

"Yes, sir." Helmut could barely finish the sentence. Seconds later, he sagged with exhaustion into a nervous semi-sleep. *Nicole?* Again his thoughts went back to her. He felt good with her. And yet, even there the world was not real, it couldn't be.

Helmut felt more than a little wary as he made his way towards the darkened little barn at the edge of an eerie field. *I don't even know this girl,* he thought to himself, wondering at the last moment if she could be a member of the Resistance or if an ambush was planned. Yet, even this knowledge did little other than compel him further. If he could expose a member of the Resistance, he would be hailed a hero!

Helmut pushed open the wooden door. The barn was part of the estate of the country house from which Nicole's uncle had been deported. The farm was extensive—plenty of room for the Resistance to hide—and Helmut felt a pang of worry when he saw that the barn was empty. But a candle was burning, and Nicole had told him to wait for her.

Sitting down on a bale of hay, Helmut took a look around. In the corner of the barn was a wooden box, partly concealed by straw. His interest piqued, Helmut walked over to the box and flipped the lid, drawing back in surprise at what he saw. He knew he should close the lid—walk away, leave this place—but he couldn't. He bent down and looked closer. In the box were a German radio and an old box of cigars, along with a tangle of suspicious cables.

"Helmut?" Nicole stood in the doorway, tears in her eyes.

A million thoughts flashed through his mind. *Is she, or perhaps someone in her family, part of the Resistance, as I thought? Has it all been a setup, an ambush, and with her weak, womanly ways she is now feeling the guilt of her betrayal?*

"Helmut… I'm sorry," she sobbed, coming toward him, tears running down her face.

"What is it?" Helmut asked, almost fearing the answer so much that he could barely stand to ask.

"You're not safe here. I mean… as a German soldier, you can't be here. You're not safe with me. It's… it's my brother." She sobbed.

"What do you mean? Nicole? Is there something you want to tell me?" Helmut asked, desperate to know the truth. He slipped his hand down to his holster to check that his gun was still there. It was.

"No, I can't. It's something my brother said, but I can't tell you what. Now, please, you have to go. Leave this place." She pushed him toward the door of the barn, and he stumbled out into the darkness.

"Tell me, Nicole," Helmut implored her. "Your brother… is he a member of the Resistance?"

Nicole said nothing, but the look on her face told him that it was true.

"And you?" he hissed into the darkness. "You too?"

Again, she said nothing but covered her face as she ran.

Fearing a sudden attack, Helmut made his way back toward the fields, toward home; his secret girlfriend had occupied his thoughts almost totally for the past few days, despite the fact that he readily admitted that he barely knew her. And now that he knew the truth about her and her family, he made a decision that for his own safety and the safety of his comrades, it would be safer for him to stay away from the French civilians for the time being, including Nicole. He couldn't trust her, and while he was now certain that her brother had something to do with the Resistance, it would be hard to prove. That box in the barn would be hidden by the time he returned with comrades. So, he would just have to bide his time and wait for the moment to strike...

Helmut awoke suddenly from his short dream. He shook his head. *That wench, what a disappointment. Like everything in this war*. He pulled himself up spit any remaining vile in his mouth out. It didn't help. He had to pull himself together, now. He had preserved his soldier's honor, he believed, and now, all he had to do was survive the rest.

Niemandsland

"Get ready for the march. We have to get out, scour the beach," the officer said as he tapped Helmut on the shoulder. "Wake up. Take the assault rifle. We have to move on ahead."

Carefully, the exhausted men picked themselves up. They didn't hear any shots. Crouching like hares, Helmut and the rest of the crew walked to the beach.

Not a hundred meters above the dunes, the first shots hit the sand. "Semi-automatic fire to the right." Helmut pressed himself flat onto the sand, recognizing in spite of the darkness, the dark stooping figures only one dune further on.

"Surround them," whispered the officer to his men. Without responding to the fire, the men managed to position themselves to the side and behind the suspected group of gunmen. But the enemy had recognized their plans and fired for all they were worth. The comrade to the left of Helmut collapsed, instantly dead with a direct hit to the face.

Singular shots became full salvos. Helmut fired off some rounds from the assault rifle. He heard his opponents screaming. Then, some single shots dropping off into silence.

Helmut moved along with his group sideways. He didn't trust this calm. Some of them could still be alive, so he fired from close range. Single shots. *Pistol shots?* Helmut tried to recognize the actions of his comrades. In fact, some gave the wounded Americans the coup de grace. Helmut shook his head, but paramedics were too far away to help the enemy soldiers anyway.

The beach was quiet. His comrades tried to help wounded Germans as far as they could. Most wounded Americans did help. Many were left to their fate.

The hours dragged on, and Helmut and his new comrades became somewhat acquainted with each other. They knew their job was not over yet. There were more snipers lurking somewhere down the beach. They decided to ambush them and render them harmless before they could sneak into their own positions. "Forward to the beach," hissed the old officer. "There, behind the iron barricades. There may still be snipers lurking there."

"It should be low tide now," added Helmut. It looked spooky. Where the now-shallow waves rolled onto the beach stood the plowed-in Rommelspargel, and tank mines planted on the posts; they looked like extra-terrestrial skeletons, like totems to deter people from approaching, and corpses lay in front of more than a few posts.

"Forward to the water's edge," ordered the old officer. "Maybe we'll find something."

The men knew what he meant, because they were not only looking for snipers but also for souvenirs. Pistols and watches were popular. Now it was low tide, so they could go far onto the beach. They had already collected some valuables, and snipers had not discovered them yet. Behind a Rommelspargel lay a half-hidden , young GI. He was wounded in the face, and his eyes closed, but he still moved.

"He's still alive," observed a soldier.

"Does he have a 1911?" asked Helmut curiously. "I could do with that as a souvenir."

Helmut approached the GI, whose face was full of mud. He poked the boy in the side with his foot, just to make sure he was not dangerous. He shook his head. Did he recognize anything about the boy?

The comrade tugged Helmut by the sleeve: "What is it? What are you waiting for?" he asked as he produced a P-38.

Helmut waved him back. "I have a strange feeling. Anyway, he's mine. I'll try being a human, at least for now." Helmut pulled the nearly unconscious man by his wet jacket ashore and left him lying in the dunes, where it was swarming with wounded people. "If the paramedics don't come soon, many won't make it. Don't we have any paramedics in the area?"

The comrade shrugged his shoulders as he set out to filch the GI soldier's jacket. "Hey, Helmut, this guy seems interesting."

Helmut pulled out a cigarette "What did you find?"

"He's got a nice fighting knife. Besides, his name tag... Didn't you say your name is Schmidt? Maybe he's related to you."

Helmut knelt beside the soldier and rubbed the dirt from the man's face. Helmut's eyes froze. It couldn't be. "I'll be damned if this boy is who I think he is."

The 20th of July

Field Marshal Rommel was in a good mood. "Speidel, you're welcome to finish early. It's too warm here in this elegant mansion, don't you think?"

"It's already late afternoon, so don't worry about me. Besides, someone might call."

"You seem to be talking on the phone all day. Are you waiting for a call, in particular?" asked the Field Marshal, slightly confused.

"I'm waiting for an important confirmation, but that's all right now."

"Really? I'm surprised. You know, after we repelled the enemy, it's become rather quiet in our Army Group. Or do you have another opinion?"

"Yes and no," said Speidel. "We should always stay on the ball, anyway."

"Do you think the Anglo-Americans will come back again? Certainly, not this year."

"There are enough other things to worry about, Herr Field Marshal. We must remain vigilant."

"Cognac, Speidel? Help yourself. You seem tense."

"I could use one. Thank you, Field Marshal."

"Now, you sit down and relax. I wanted to talk to you about something."

Nervously, Speidel adjusted his leather chair, and Field Marshal Rommel sat down in front of his desk.

Rommel looked incredulously at his general. "What do you think? Were we lucky or did the new strategy actually work?"

Speidel emptied the glass with one sip, paused for a few seconds, and felt better immediately. He cleared his throat. "Well, a great strategist without luck is a worthless strategist, Field Marshal."

"Frederick the Great, I know. But seriously, do you think the focus on small arms and abandoning the completion of the originally planned large bunkers with their heavy guns was ultimately the catalyst for our success?"

"I'm sure that was the best strategy given the circumstances and our possibilities."

Rommel nodded. "I think so too. Of course, we can't know 100%. And if the Allies had used more naval guns, which the English, in contrast to the Americans, almost completely neglected, then I don't know."

"Fantasy helps as well, Herr Field Marshal."

Rommel kept glancing at Speidel. He had been on the phone a lot today. The Field Marshal could feel something in the air. "Speidel, you've been restless all morning. Now, shoot; what is on your mind?"

Speidel wiped the sweat from his forehead. "It's really hot today; that's all."

"You're right. You should still take it easy. Enjoy the days Speidel. You have just been awarded a distinction. You were the one who repelled the landing."

"Well, not exactly, Herr Field Marshal, I simply followed your orders."

"Don't be so modest, Speidel. I was on vacation. And you reacted correctly."

"May I ask you something, Herr Rommel?"

"Go for it!"

"What do you think of the enemy now?"

"Well, I have to say that the huge material superiority and air domination from the very disciplined Americans have not made it easy for us. Of course, a little luck was part of it as well."

"And which weapons were most effective in your opinion?"

"Look, Speidel, the Allies are playing the war of the rich man. We have much less at our disposal, but it was still possible for us to win.

But the English also have an excellent fighting spirit, especially in close combat. Naturally, the Englishmen were very different, sometimes generous, sometimes killers, depending on where they landed.

Speidel shrugged nervously. His grin seemed artificial. The nervousness of the Colonel-General didn't escape Rommel either.

"Very well, Speidel, what do you think the Anglo-Americans will do? Are they coming again?"

"No, Field Marshal, I don't believe so, at least not this year."

"So?"

"Well, I suppose they will muddle their way through and won't do anything for now."

Rommel sipped his cup. "Something is up today, I'm telling you."

No sooner had Rommel finished speaking than the telephone rang. Speidel jumped up from his chair. "Field-Marshal, I'll answer."

Rommel heard his Chief of Staff give only short, stubborn-sounding answers on the phone. Then, Speidel fell quiet,

"Speidel, you look so pale. What's going on?"

"Field Marshal, it's General von Stuelpnagel for you."

Slowly, with an incredulous face, Rommel took the receiver. "Yes, Rommel here... An assassination attempt on the Fuehrer?... Are you sure?... You want WHAT from me?"

Stunned and speechless Field Marshal Rommel put the phone down. He leaned back deep in his wing chair. "The Fuehrer is dead... I'm sure you want to tell me something, Speidel."

After a few seconds of silence, Speidel leaned forward. "Field Marshal, I've known you long enough. You must have guessed. The enemy holds you in high esteem. Everyone knows that. Take over the leadership of the Reich. The Oberkommando West is already waiting for you and will follow you."

***

126

Author Note

It is well-known that the High Command of the Wehrmacht placed great value on strategic panzer reserves, which in the event of an Allied landing were to capture and destroy their troops throughout France. Rommel was one of the few influential commanders who realized that such a strategy was doomed to

failure due to the total Allied air superiority. Again and again, he tried to assert his strategy to make the beach the main battle line to the High Command of the Wehrmacht; yet, in reality, he didn't succeed because the most important armored forces in Normandy were kept in reserve by Hitler personally.

Indeed, there were all sorts of intrigues against Rommel, who, as the youngest Field Marshal of the Reich, was also accompanied by alternating war fortunes throughout his career. He also aroused the envy and resentment of many high-ranking generals and Nazis. This novel should also reflect this handicap of Rommel's, as well as his alternative approach, which he did implement, but only to a very limited extent.

Rommel never managed to assert himself against the official strategy of his superiors. And his influence as a commissioner for the completion of the Atlantic Wall was also very limited. It is true that the Army command and also Hitler himself were accurately informed by the Air Force and Navy, but they came too late to the conclusion that the presumed amassing of enemy troops at Dover was a decoy and that Normandy, with an assured certain likelihood, would become the predetermined landing pad.

Many of the leading Generals, including von Rundstedt, fiercely resisted any changes. The introduction of new and numerous small arms was a well-known theoretical aspect that would normally have been taken for granted, but there were individual commanders, such as Rommel's hardest adversaries, e.g., General von Schweppenburg, who, to some extent, took it into consideration. Nevertheless, it resulted only in theoretical games; in reality, none of these ideas were implemented to the extent necessary.

This novel, which, of course, also contains many fantasy elements, such as soldier experiences and battle scenes, is a dotted attempt to show what could have been, especially if Rommel could have implemented more of his ideas – this and the well-known idea to use new small arms on a massive scale on the coastal front. That Rommel knew about the attempted assassination of July 20th has been well-documented. The novel briefly shows that he trusted Speidel and also that had the assassination succeeded, regardless of the outcome of the landing, Rommel had a cautious nature both as a General and as a man.

***

D-DAY REPULSED

Thanks for reading the book, see more of Claude's military novels:
www.claudestahl.com

CLAUDE STAHL
SS VICTORY
IN
THE WEST
THE BATTLE OF THE BULGE • AGAINST ALL ODDS
A NOVEL

SS Victory in the West

The Battle of the Bulge

Against all Odds

The Sound of Tanks

"We shoot the white helmets first: they're the SS." First Sergeant Mitch McGraw always meant what he said. In Normandy, he had retaliated just as he had promised. That was four months ago, and since then, the war had shaped him, leaving its mark on his face. It showed bitterness, suffering, hardship. His greasy black hair brushed the collar of his over-sized field jacket, which hid his battered body and gave him protection from the cold.

He remembered the first time he'd met the bastards of the Hitler Youth Division. During the reconnaissance advance behind Caen, they had appeared out of nowhere: his squad had been roaming through the confusing bocage hedgerows for almost two days when the Halftracks broke through the bushes. Escape was futile: outgunned by the German mounted flak Vierling, they stood no chance.

The devils were only around seventeen. Their helmets were covered with camouflage nets; only the SS did that. His men raised their hands; many were simply too surprised and exhausted to play heroes, so they surrendered, submitted as the Germans shouted at them, gave orders in German – and suddenly the banging started. McGraw jumped through the bushes in one bound, and pressed himself deep into the woods. Seconds later, most of his men were shot to pieces. One of them had only been shot in the legs; he was whimpering and spinning on the ground in pain. An SS brat knelt down in front of him and stole his 45 as a souvenir, leaving the wounded man to bleed to death. They didn't care about the GIs. They got back into their vehicles and drove on.

McGraw couldn't do anything more for his men. Late that night, he joined a supply unit heading for Caen, and the next morning, on the old main road to Dieppe, he saw the same German Halftracks, this time almost obliterated in rubble and ash. They had been annihilated by fighter bombers – yet some of the murderers still had life enough to groan. They lay in a wet ditch, perhaps half a dozen still breathing. McGraw ran to the truck and, drawing protests from the other soldiers, pulled down a can of gasoline. He gripped it, deaf to the objections of his group. It had to be done and it was meant to be done. He crested the top of the ditch and sloshed gasoline over the screaming, pleading wounded. The match felt hot in his hand, but strangely, after he started the fire, the Krauts hardly screamed at all. It must have been the choking, oily smoke; the bastards must have suffocated before the flames reached their skin.

Time doesn't heal all wounds. Recalling those SS bastards still angered him. The war had become thought and memory, yet he knew exactly where he was, and his upcoming task seemed clearer than ever. Here they stood, he the so-called veteran, who had worked himself up to driver and gunner and now first sergeant; and his men, who were not comrades or friends, but a sort of family, at his back. This morning, he didn't want to go too far away from headquarters. It could be over at any time, he was sure, but to move among the men was good for nerves and morale. The man lay around like vagabonds, but McGraw was proud of them: these were the conquerors of the first German soil. Since Normandy, many had died, but some of his old comrades had been rotated home with self-inflicted injuries, and quite a few had managed to get transferred back to the supply troops – not him, though.

He pulled his helmet low and leaned his M1 against the sandbags. Time was running out. He had to find out first-hand how soon the artillery positions would be ready, and whether the Paks were in the right place, because if it started and orders came, he wanted to be prepared. After all, the enemy forces were still considerable, and this was the just-conquered city of Aachen, the first big city that the supposedly Thousand-Year-Reich had lost to the west. The enemy was staggered and defeated, but he was not yet dead. Just yesterday, McGraw's squad had cleaned the center of the last hidden Krauts, and then – just in case the enemy should get any stupid ideas about taking back the city – they had marched another 10 kilometers to the outskirts, to secure the rail and road junction, which stood on the border of three countries, in the ruins of a railway station. They needed to stay active and alert even now.

However, something – or someone – was standing in the way of his work. There he stood now, like a mismatched stone in a wall. The naive and pompous reporter Henry George, of Time Magazine – who had accompanied him since the liberation of Paris, or better, who had found him again and again, and whom he could neither stand nor get rid of – always wanted just one thing: a story delivered. All McGraw could do was show him reality. "Didn't know there was an SS stationed here at the front near Aachen."

"You couldn't have, either; they arrived last night."

George shook his head. "Shouldn't there be German infantry behind that railroad embankment?"

"Like I said, they switched people. We found out yesterday that there are parts of the 12th Panzer somewhere nearby, so we're going to be dealing with the Hitler Youth Division."

George tried to make out something through the field glass, but the white horizon showed no movement. "Since it snowed, you can't see a thing."

McGraw just nodded and tugged the collar of his army jacket up to his helmet, then rubbed his hands and put a lump of weed in his mouth.

"If we can't see, the Krauts can't see, right, Sergeant?

McGraw spat in the snow, irritated. "Probably, but there's movement behind the trees and the sheds."

Again, George tried to make out something, without success. "What is that, cursed spirits?"

Now McGraw took up the field glasses. "This morning, we heard the sound of tanks."

Young George shook slightly. It wasn't so much the cold and snowdrifts as the iron wind that snarled through every gap in his uniform; he had to get out of here. No point in standing around in this filthy weather; there wasn't news here either; the whole thing was a miserable state of affairs. "So back to the barracks now, Sergeant?"

"You want to break up? The day has just begun."

George wiped his mouth and looked sideways at the sergeant. "Hell of a way to celebrate our holiday."

McGraw spat out the weed he was chewing. "Holiday of what?"

"It's November 23rd. There's foodstuff from France in our barracks."

McGraw shrugged. "All the good stuff still comes all the way from France. It's a very long way, you know?"

"Why is that?"

"Antwerp port is still not cleared, full of mines."

"I loved France. Not this hassle here."

McGraw pulled out a flask without taking his eyes off the horizon. A short, hasty swallow. "The bastards are up to something, I tell you."

"You think they're expecting us yet?"

"They're not expecting us; they are coming for us."

SS Victory in the West - The Battle of the Bulge

Now available on all major book platforms.

***

www.ingramcontent.com/pod-product-compliance
Lightning Source LLC
Chambersburg PA
CBHW071940210726
48293CB00004BA/1317